Arpeggio took off like an express train and came blasting down the path. Dara maneuvered him onto the grass and directed him toward the jump. Several strides before the dip, she gripped his sides more firmly with her legs and shifted her weight forward slightly, usually the only incentive he needed to leave the ground in a graceful arc and clear whatever obstacle was directly in front of him.

But this time there was nothing directly in front of him. The jump, which he could see clearly, was several strides away. By the way Arpeggio moved, Dara knew he was confused. If he jumped this little dip in the ground and then landed, he'd crash right into the jump. It was too late, but Dara saw that taking this jump had been a stupid, grandstand play. Changing her mind, she tried to halt Arpeggio's forward motion, but it was no good.

Dara was thrown from the saddle. Arpeggio faltered and came down just short of the brush pile. His eyes rolled in his head as he tried to extricate his feet from the branches and leaves. Thrashing about wildly, he finally freed himself and took off like a streak down the trail, the sound of his hooves fading away, one broken rein flying over his shoulder. For a minute there was total silence, even the cicadas were stunned into quiet. . . .

Other Fawcett Girls Only Titles:

BLUE RIBBON #4
GOLDEN GIRL

Chris St. John

FAWCETT GIRLS ONLY • NEW YORK

RLI: $\dfrac{\text{VL 5 \& up}}{\text{II 6 \& up}}$

A Fawcett Girls Only Book
Published by Ballantine Books
Copyright © 1989 by Cloverdale Press, Inc.

Library of Congress Catalog Card Number: 89-91130

ISBN 0-449-13454-7

Printed in Canada

First Edition: September 1989

Chapter 1

THE August sun had been up less than an hour, but already the air was hot. Dara Cooper released the pressure of her legs against the sides of the gray gelding she was riding, and eased the tension on the reins. Arpeggio slowed immediately from a trot to a walk. Dara let the reins slide through her hands until they hung in a casual loop from the bit to her fingers. Gratefully, the big gray lowered his head and relaxed.

The woods were very quiet and misty. It seemed to Dara that except for her and Arpeggio, the whole world was still asleep. Dara knew a weather man would explain the morning mist as the humidity of a late New England summer, but Dara preferred thinking of the soft look of the woods as something magical.

"Good morning, woods," she said in her husky voice. "I'm back!" She tossed her head so that her short, heavy blond hair fanned out around her face and her slightly tilted nose and deep blue

1

eyes. She'd lived in Smithfield, Connecticut, for only a few months, but the town and the woods around it felt more like home than anyplace she'd ever been.

She breathed in the sweet air and felt some of the tension leave her body. For all of July she and Kate Wiley, a friend who loved riding as much as she did, had been in Vermont at Tommy Langwald's training camp, learning to be better, stronger combined training riders. They'd gotten back only yesterday.

Eventing was probably the most difficult competition in the horse world. To succeed in it you had to have a horse that was supple enough to perform the precise gymnastic moves necessary for dressage, a horse that would listen carefully to every little thing you told him and obey your instructions instantly. That same horse had to have the stamina to complete several endurance tests, including a cross-country course. He had to have the strength, courage, and agility to carry his rider safely over hedges, ditches, fallen logs, and anything else he came up against on the outside course, and do it faster than any other horse running that day. And then, when he was tired and strung out from the excitement, he had to have enough energy and obedience left to go over a series of jumps cleanly, quietly, and competently in the show ring in the final phase of eventing.

The month of training at Tommy's had been intense and exhausting, and hadn't ended as well as Dara had hoped it would. She'd come in second to Kate in the competition that ended their training. Night Owl, Kate's horse, had had one of his better days. She bit her lower lip and told herself second wasn't so bad, it was just a position Dara hadn't found herself in very often. If she *had* to come in second, she guessed Kate was the person she'd least mind coming in second to. But Dara's mother thought anything less than a blue ribbon was a failure. Dara sighed. Her mother had made only one oblique reference to the fact that Kate had beaten her, but Dara knew she hadn't forgotten. Nor had she forgotten the agreement she'd exacted from Dara when they'd bought Arpeggio. "As long as you win," Mrs. Cooper had told her daughter, "he's yours."

Arpeggio stopped and his ears pricked forward. His head was high and Dara could see his nostrils working the air. "What do you see?" she asked him softly. "Are there deer out there?" he snorted, and shook his head. Dara peered between the trees, where the sun's rays made long columns of light, but she saw nothing. After another minute of concentration Arpeggio lowered his head and walked on.

She reached down and ran a hand along Arpeggio's withers, feeling his muscles extend and contract as he walked. His skin was like warm satin, and she felt a rush of love and affection for the horse. What would she ever do without him? She almost bent down to place a kiss on his neck, but held herself back. Kissing horses was something Kate did. Dara had learned early on, almost in self-defense, not to give in to the feelings she had for Arpeggio. Sometimes she felt that he was only on loan to her. But here she was on this beautiful morning so filled with happiness and love that she had to do something, and who would see if—for once—she lost her cool? Nobody. So, bending forward, she gave Arpeggio a loud, smacking kiss. The noise startled the horse and he flicked back his ears, listening. Dara laughed at her silliness.

"Are you as happy here as I am?" she asked. "I'll bet you are. I'll bet you like it at Windcroft a lot better than you did at Concordia." Concordia was the stable in Pennsylvania where Arpeggio had been kept before the Cooper family moved to Smithfield. "Night Owl and Time-Out are great pals, aren't they? Not like those snooty horses you used to hang around with." Night Owl and Time-Out were Kate Wiley's and Jessie Robeson's horses and Arpeggio's stablemates. Kate and Jessie were the best friends Dara had ever had.

Dara stopped to think about how wonderful it was that the three girls could ride, and compete against each other, and still be friends, real friends, with no secrets between them, and no backbiting in the ring. Dara had always suspected that half the kids at Concordia were just waiting for her to blow it. But she never did. Dara thought sometimes that she and Arpeggio were touched with magic. Her brother Matt called her the Golden Girl.

Thinking of Matt caused Dara to remember that her favorite brother was coming home today. And if things weren't perfect enough, there was Doug. Filled suddenly with a fierce happiness at the thought of Doug, Dara bent down to hug Arpeggio's neck again. "I like him more than any boy

I've ever gone out with," she whispered to her horse.

They came to the stream that meandered through the woods and Arpeggio stopped to take a drink. When he raised his dripping muzzle, Dara turned him around and headed him slowly home.

Rocking gently in the saddle, Dara let her mind wander to the day ahead of her. Jessie and Kate would be coming for lunch. They were going to hang out in the pool until suppertime and catch up. Jessie hadn't gone to Langwald's camp and was dying to hear all that had happened there. Dara grinned at the thought of filling Jessie in. She and Kate could make a lot of what happened seem funny—even the part about Dara coming in second to Kate. They'd laugh and joke about all their experiences, and forget about any bad times.

And then, after dinner she had a date with Doug, the first one in a month. He hadn't come up to Vermont with the rest of the gang to see the camp horse trials. Jessie said he'd wanted to but he couldn't. Well, she was home now, and they'd be able to spend the rest of the summer together, that is, they could if he felt the same way about her as she did about him.

"I guess that about fills up today," she said with a satisfied grin.

"And then," Dara said to Jessie in her sultry, lazy voice, "he looked at me and said, 'No one is perfect,' after he'd just spent ten minutes telling us *he* was!" Her blue eyes, which were normally bright enough to make people look at them twice, now blazed as if they were neon.

The girls were stretched out in the sun on the patio around the pool in Dara's backyard. Kate laughed, and reached for the suntan lotion. "He was a character, all right," she agreed. She and Dara were talking about Tommy Langwald. Kate coated her legs with the lotion, and then lay back on her chaise, lifting her long blond hair off her neck, her gray-green eyes sparkling with remembering.

Jessie sat on the stone coping above the pool, her feet paddling the water, making a cool splashing sound and sending glistening drops into the air.

"Don't you wish now that you had gone?" Dara asked. "Then you'd have a month's worth of horror stories too."

"Not for one second," Jessie said, grinning, her warm hazel eyes taking in her two closest friends. She hooked her shoulder-length brown hair behind one ear. "The first time he yelled at me I'd have started to cry and run for home."

"And he certainly did yell," Dara said.

"He certainly did," Kate agreed, the smile leaving her face.

Dara looked at Kate and could tell that something was bothering her. She remembered an incident that had happened at the camp after the last competition. Tommy Langwald had called Kate into his office, and Kate had come out looking upset.

"Listen, Kate," Dara had said. "Don't let him bother you. Some coaches think that yelling a lot is a good way to get you motivated."

"Well, that kind of coaching doesn't work with me," Kate had said.

Still, for all his lack of tact, Dara had learned a lot. She thought "old Fangwald" was pretty smart when it came to horses and riders.

Kate had disagreed. "Maybe he's smart about riders," she'd muttered, "but not about horses."

"Are you still moping about things he said to you?" Dara asked, adjusting her position on the chaise so that more of her legs were in the sun. "You have to give him some credit, he got you to the point where you could beat me," she teased. "And anyone who can fix it so someone beats me must be pretty good."

"Don't you love modesty?" Jessie asked Kate.

"Actually," Kate said, grinning, "I think you threw the match. What was the matter with you? You looked like your mind was on vacation."

"Some vacation," Dara groaned.

But there was a ring of truth to what Kate said. Dara hadn't been paying attention that last afternoon. The wrap-up competition had been held on the last day, the same day that the whole gang from Smithfield had come up to see them, except for Doug. Dara had been terribly hurt but kept it to herself.

He'd had a tennis match to play, Jessie'd said. He'd wanted to come but couldn't. Dara of all people should understand that. How many times had she had to say no to Doug because of her riding? She had been so disappointed, she'd found it hard to concentrate on anything, let alone dressage. And perhaps her lapse of attention in the ring that day was understandable considering how important Doug had become to her, but she couldn't risk doing it again. Every lapse meant risking Arpeggio, and Arpeggio was important to her too.

"What's with you, Cooper?" Kate asked.

Dara came back to the present with a jolt and looked at Kate quickly. "Nothing," she said.

"Are you sure? You looked kind of funny for a minute."

Dara looked at her cross-eyed. "It's this heat. I think my brains are fried."

"Could someone explain to me why we are out here roasting when there's this big pool of cool water right here under my feet?" Jessie asked.

Dara stood up and stretched. "There's no explaining some things," she said in a deep, mysterious voice. Then she stepped to the edge of the pool, adjusted the straps of her purple-and-white print bathing suit, and dove in. She plunged to the bottom of the pool, then pushed with her hands so that she surfaced at the other end. She tossed her head to clear the water from her eyes and lay back floating. The sun was warm on her face and the water cool against her back. Turning over, she struck out strongly, swimming to the side of the pool, and sent a huge splash of water over Jessie and Kate.

Jessie screamed in shock. "Listen," she said, "you can hear it sizzle on my arm. Oh, this feels wonderful." She got up, ran back to the edge of the patio, then headed straight for the pool and did a cannonball, sending an explosion of water high into the air. "Come on, Kate, you'll love it."

When they were all in the water, Kate suggested they do a water ballet. They lay out on the water, their feet almost touching, kicking them until there was a circle of white foam between them. Then they did the backstroke until they touched the sides of the pool, dove under backward, and resurfaced a few feet from each other in the center.

"I'll bet that looks great from the deck," Jessie said, "just like those water nymphs in those shows in Florida."

"Hey, maybe if we don't make the Olympic Equestrian Team, we have a chance for fame and fortune in the Everglades," Kate said, and laughed.

"My mother would not be satisfied with a water nymph for a daughter," Dara said. "It's the Olympic Equestrian Team or bust, for me."

"Your mom is really bent on you making the Olympics, isn't she," Kate said, pushing her wet hair out of her eyes.

"Isn't your mom?" Dara asked her. Kate's family owned Windcroft Stables, where the girls kept their horses, and Kate's mother, Anne Wiley, was their coach.

"I guess," Kate said quietly.

Dara knew what she was thinking. No mother in the whole world was more intent on her daughter making the Olympics than Mrs. Cooper was.

"Hey, did I tell you guys what my mom is forcing me to do?" Kate said, changing the subject. Kate treaded water and looked unhappy. "She says I have to ride Northern Spy at Waterfall Farm in the next competition."

Northern Spy was a horse that belonged to Pietro Yon, a friend of the Wiley family. Mr. Yon had been Mrs. Wiley's coach when she was competing. He recently had to give up his own farm for health reasons, and he'd sold all of his horses except Northern Spy. He asked the Wileys if they would keep Spy until the right owner was found for him.

"How come you have to ride Spy?" Jessie asked as she did a slow breaststroke.

"Because we promised Mr. Yon we'd get Spy around to the horse trials so that people could see him and maybe buy him ... if old Pietro thinks they're good enough. Remember? That was supposed to have been your job," Kate said to Jessie. Jessie's horse, Time-Out, had been expecting a foal, and Kate had thought it would solve everybody's problems if Jessie rode Spy. But the combination of Jessie and Spy hadn't been a success. "Why don't you try riding him again," Kate coaxed Jessie. "If you would ride him at Waterfall, my mom would get off my back."

"Take my life in my hands riding Spy again?" Jessie said. "I believe in friends doing favors for friends, but there are limits. And don't try to make me feel guilty," Jessie said, sounding guilty. "It was your idea that I ride Spy in the first place. I can't help it if he turned out to be too advanced for me."

Kate glared menacingly at Jessie, who sank slowly under the water so that she wouldn't have to meet Kate's eyes. Dara reached underwater to pull Jessie back up.

"Do you know how upset Night Owl is going to be when we all get ready to go to Waterfall and he has to stay home?" Kate asked. "He'll go into one of his depressions."

Dara stared at Kate and wondered if Mrs. Wiley

had an ulterior motive in getting Kate to ride Spy. Dara had a sneaking suspicion that the reason Spy ended up at Windcroft was for Kate. Maybe Mrs. Wiley was trying to force Kate to see what a great horse Spy was. If that was her plan, it was a good idea, because Kate showed no signs of discovering that fact on her own. She was too wrapped up in Night Owl. So wrapped up that she refused to see that he wasn't talented enough to take her where she wanted to go.

"Tell you what," Dara said. "We can't have Big Bird moping in a stall all by himself. Why don't we all go to Waterfall and Jessie can ride the Owl?"

Jessie stared at Dara blankly for a minute and Dara stared back at her, trying to signal her to go along. She succeeded because suddenly a light seemed to go on in Jessie's head. "That's a great idea," she said, trying to sound enthused.

"It is?" Kate asked.

"Sure," Jessie said, warming a little to the idea. "The Owl and I are old friends."

"I thought you didn't like to compete," Kate said suspiciously. "I thought that's why you bought Time-Out. So you wouldn't have all that blue-ribbon anxiety."

"I don't like to compete at the level you guys are at," Jessie said. "But I do like going to horse trials and doing things in my own slow way. Time-Out won't be ready for me to take to an event for months yet. She just had her colt in May. I miss the excitement and the fun of going to events with a horse."

Kate looked at both of them for a long time. "Is

this some kind of conspiracy? Did my mom put you up to this?"

"I haven't spoken to your mom in a month," Dara said.

"Well," Kate said, and then sighed. "Okay."

"Great," Jessie said, slapping a spray of water up into the air.

Dara had observed Night Owl for some time now. He was a wonderful horse, but he wasn't dependable, and it was those times that Kate lost ribbons. Spy, on the other hand, was one of the steadiest, most competitive horses Dara had ever seen. Kate on Night Owl was beatable. Kate on Spy might be a different story. Somehow Dara knew that her mother was not going to be happy with this turn of events. It would probably be better not to tell her.

A funny feeling wormed its way through Dara. She didn't like keeping secrets from her mother. Bad as things had sometimes been in Lancaster, she'd always been able to tell her mother everything. Since moving to Smithfield, something had changed. Dara couldn't quite put her finger on what it was. But whatever it was, her mother was much less understanding than she had been, and she kept bringing up the agreement Dara had made about Arpeggio.

"Can we stop talking horses now," Dara asked, turning her attention back to her friends, "and get back to being water nymphs?"

"Fine with me," Jessie said. "I'm better at this nymph business anyway."

They repeated their little ballet routine, but this time when Dara swam backward away from the froth of water their kicking feet had created, she heard the sound of applause.

She reached the side of the pool and twisting quickly, she looked up and gave a happy scream. "Matt," she said, "I almost forgot you were coming."

"Great," Matt said, touch of sarcasm in his voice. He looked at the other two girls. "That kind of welcome just warms me through and through."

Dara swam to the ladder and climbed out of the water. "Well, I mean ... I remembered this morning, but then ... ah, never mind. You're here, and that's great!" Dara exclaimed.

"No hug?" Matt asked Dara.

"I'm soaking wet," Dara said.

"It'll feel great, like a giant ice cube," Matt said, grabbing his sister around her waist and lifting her several inches off the ground before putting her down again.

"Kate, Jessie," Dara said, combing her wet hair out of her eyes and smiling broadly, "this is my brother Matt."

The girls said hello and Jessie asked if he'd been away on a trip. "Nope," Matt said. "I had to take a couple of courses this summer because my marks weren't what they should have been. Yale's funny that way," he said, grinning. "They like passing grades."

He looked around the backyard and then at the white colonial house with its bright blue awnings. "Not bad," he said.

"That's right," Kate said. "This is the first time you've seen it."

Matt looked at his sister. "So, how does it compare to Lancaster?"

"I like it lots better," Dara said.

"The house is smaller," Matt said.

"Smaller?" Jessie said. "This is the biggest house in Smithfield."

"Well," Matt said, smiling, "Smithfield is definitely not Lancaster."

"Thank heavens for that," Dara said emphatically.

"Is Mom home?" Matt asked, looking toward the house again.

"She's playing golf," Dara told him.

His face brightened. "Great, then I get a reprieve."

"Matt?" Dara said. "Is she going to be upset with you?"

"Upset with me?" Matt asked, feigning innocence. "Not possible."

Dara laughed. "I'm glad you're home," she said, standing on tiptoe and kissing his cheek. "Go get changed and we can play water polo."

He sat down on one of the chairs, took off his Docksiders, stripped off his shirt, and said, "Consider me changed, shorts are as good as a bathing suit any day. Which one of you lucky ladies gets me for a partner?"

"Me," Dara said, holding his arm possessively. "They'll have to get their own big brother."

They played until they were breathless, and then lounged in the shallow end of the pool talking until they heard a car door slam. "That must be Mom," Dara said.

"Well, I hope Mom welcomes me with open arms," Matt said, and Dara thought she saw a nervous glint in his eye.

Dara watched as he hoisted himself out of the pool and headed for the house. "Matt," she called after him. "We're all glad that you're home."

"Thanks." He grinned at her as he grabbed a towel.

After he disappeared through the back door, Kate said, "Don't take this the wrong way, Dara, but never in a million years would I guess that Matt was your brother."

"Me either," Jessie said. "He's nice, and good-looking, but somehow I thought a Cooper male would be more sophisticated."

"You're describing my two older brothers, the one in med school and the one who's a lawyer. Matt is"—and she smiled fondly—"just Matt." She looked up at the sky, "Well, if Mom's home it must be close to five. Are you guys going to ride?" she asked.

Kate looked at Jessie. "I guess I might as well get started on Spy. Do you want to come over tonight and ride the Owl?" She stopped herself and asked her friends, "Why did I agree to this?"

They just laughed at Kate and continued their conversation. "Are you riding with us tonight?" Jessie asked Dara.

"Nope," Dara said. "Tonight I have a date with Doug."

"You guys are like a fairy tale," Jessie said. It was a sincere compliment with no jealous undertones.

"Sometimes that's what my life feels like," Dara confided to her friend with a smile.

Chapter 2

DARA was hoping that the conversation at the dinner table would center around polite requests to pass the salt, but she wasn't that lucky. When Dara handed the crystal shaker to her mother, Mrs. Cooper's next question was "How did your training with Arpeggio go?"

"Fine," Dara said, cutting her chicken breast carefully.

"What did you work on?"

"Nothing much," Dara said, avoiding her mother's gaze.

"Nothing much?" Mrs. Cooper paused with a fork halfway to her mouth.

"I took him out on the trails this morning while it was still cool. We did some interval training," Dara said, turning their strictly-for-fun time into a schooling maneuver that her mother would approve of.

"Interval training?" Matt said, grinning at his sister. "Sounds pretty intense to me."

"Sometimes it is pretty intense," Dara said. "You don't realize what really hard work riding a horse is."

"Spare me," Matt said. "Nothing you do is hard work."

Matt's half-kidding comment referred back to their childhood, when Dara had always seemed to do things faster and better than he did. Before Dara could answer him, Mrs. Cooper asked, "What about the half-passes? I thought you were going to work on them?"

"Now, that sounds like football," Matt said after chewing a mouthful of chicken. "How in the world do you manage a half-pass on a horse?"

"It's a very complicated maneuver," Mrs. Cooper answered. "The horse has to move across the ring, facing forward, but going sideways at an angle, and crossing his legs, one over the other." She placed her right arm over her left arm so that they made an X. "Like that."

"Good heavens," Mr. Cooper said, looking at Dara. "You can get that animal to do that?"

"That animal's name is Arpeggio," Mrs. Cooper said, "and Dara can get him to do anything."

Matt caught Dara's eye, and they both laughed. It was another old joke between them, the intense interest Mrs. Cooper had in Dara's riding. She had always been interested, but lately Dara thought her mom was getting carried away, and she was becoming ... a problem. Dara was immediately sorry for the disloyal thought. "We worked on them a little in the ring, but I have plenty of time to teach him that, Mom," she said, answering her mother's question. "It won't come up in any of my dressage tests for quite a while."

Mr. Cooper smiled at his daughter. "If anyone can get a horse to do a half-pass, I'll bet you can," he said, shaking his head. Then he turned his attention to his youngest son. "It's good having you home, Matthew. How do you like our new house?"

"I like it a lot. It has a comfortable feeling," Matt said. "I always thought of the place in Pennsylvania as cold."

"I did too," Dara chimed in. "This is much more like home."

"Lancaster was home too," Mrs. Cooper said. Dara looked at her, quickly sensing a note of sadness. Did Mrs. Cooper miss Lancaster? Dara wondered what in the world she could miss about Lancaster.

"And how did the summer courses go?" Mr. Cooper asked Matt.

"Fine," Matt said too quickly, and Dara glanced in his direction. "I passed them all."

There was a silence at the table. "Passed is rather a vague report," Mr. Cooper commented.

"You might as well know straight out," Matt told his father. "I'm pretty sure I didn't get A's. I'm a little doubtful about whether I got B's," he added under his breath so that only Dara heard him.

"I suppose what you're telling us is you earned a C in those two makeup courses. Are you satisfied with those marks?" Matt refused to meet his father's eyes. "Well, if you are satisfied with doing mediocre work, then you can look forward to a mediocre life. You get only what you give, you know," his father lectured.

"Look at your sister," Mrs. Cooper chimed in. "She gives her all to everything she does, and look at what she's achieved. She's a straight-A student, she's the best rider in the state, and she's dating the most popular boy at Smithfield High. And," Mrs. Cooper went on while Dara cringed, "that's why she's been able to keep a horse like Arpeggio, and a car of her own. She's earned them."

"Mother, please," Dara said. She hated it when they came down hard on Matt. She especially hated it when they compared her to him, even though it seemed to her that Matt brought a lot of the criticism on himself. If he'd just get more serious about his work, she was sure he'd get the kind of marks that would make her parents happy. Then they'd get off his back. She loved Matt and hated to feel they were rivals.

"That's okay, Dara," Matt said, smiling philosophically. "After all, you are the Golden Girl and I am the black sheep. Together we make the Cooper family exciting." Then he leaned over to ask her with sincere interest, "*Are* you the best rider in the state?"

"No," she said.

"Who's better?" her mother asked quickly.

Dara ignored her mother's question. "I'm *not* the best rider in the state," she insisted, then added wickedly, "I'm the best rider in the whole world."

Matt groaned. "And she had to turn out to be my sister."

"But I'm also lovable and a good friend," she said, batting her eyes comically at her brother.

"That's what saves you," he said.

"Go ahead and joke about it," Mrs. Cooper said. "You'll find out that life isn't all fun and games. Do you have any plans for tonight?" she asked Dara.

"I've got a date with Doug."

"Just don't get in too late. You ought to ride early in the morning these days, before it gets too hot. When is your next lesson?"

"Thursday," Dara said.

"I have an appointment that morning, but maybe I can see some of it. Make sure you get something out of it."

"I always do," Dara said quietly.

Upstairs in her bedroom, Dara put the final touches on her makeup. Not that she wore much, just a bit of eye shadow and some lipstick. She wished she had remembered to ask Doug where they were going tonight so she'd know what to wear. She wanted to look perfect for him.

She rifled through her closet and finally decided on a pair of stone-washed denim shorts and an oversize white T-shirt that set off her tan. The doorbell rang, and she was halfway down the stairs, her heart beating like a hammer, before she got hold of herself and forced herself to slow down. "Hi," she said, smiling at Doug when she reached the bottom step. He stood in the hallway chatting with her mother.

"Hi," he said, smiling back at her.

Her insides turned all mushy. He looked so wonderful, and she had missed him so much. Of course he looks wonderful, Dara thought. After all, he's the star quarterback on the football team and a summer tennis champ. No wonder he's tanned and muscular, he's a real athlete. But those warm brown eyes are what turn me into soft ice cream!

"Well, where are you two off to?" Mrs. Cooper asked, bringing Dara down from cloud nine.

"I'm not sure," Doug said. "I was thinking we could play miniature golf, but it looks like rain. Maybe we'll go to a movie."

"Have fun," she told them as she closed the front door. "And, Dara, remember, don't get home too late."

Doug grabbed Dara's hand as they walked to the car. "They always say that," he said, laughing, as he settled himself behind the wheel.

"Don't get home too late?" Dara said. "I know."

"Well, I guess parents have to give directions or they don't feel like parents." Doug sat staring at her with a happy expression on his face.

"What are you looking at?" she asked, turning to see if there was anything behind her that was making him laugh.

"You," he said. "You look great."

"Thanks." Dara felt herself blushing. "So where *are* we going?" she asked, to change the subject.

As if in answer to her question there was a low rumble of thunder.

"Miniature golf?" Doug asked doubtfully, looking out the window.

"Sure," Dara said. "It's not going to rain on our first night out together in a month."

"It wouldn't dare," Doug said, and started the engine and drove to the Putt-Putt Golf Course.

"How good are you at this?" Doug asked suspiciously as they picked up their clubs and balls.

"Little ol' me?" Dara said. "I can't hit a golf ball to save my life."

"I think I'm in trouble," Doug moaned. "That's what you said about hitting a tennis ball, and you almost beat me silly."

Dara set her bright blue golf ball on the tee. "I wasn't telling the truth then," she said, giggling. "In Pennsylvania we belonged to the country club and I did play tennis once or twice—"

"A week, I bet," Doug cut in.

Dara sighted along her golf club as if it were a rifle aimed at the passageway between the feet of an oversize duck that stood between the tee and the hole.

"I hate to tell you this," Doug said, watching her, "but that's not a rifle, you can't shoot the ball in. You have to tap it, like this." He bumped her out of the way, put his ball on the tee, and sent it down the approach. It knocked against the duck and rolled to a stop in a corner, giving him a difficult second shot.

"Aww," Dara said. "That's too bad." She went back to sighting along the golf club. "Got it," she said finally, replaced her ball, tapped it lightly just a little off to one side, and watched while it rolled perfectly between the duck's feet and plopped into the hole beyond them.

It took Doug three more strokes to sink the ball. "That's okay, Cooper," he said. "I'm a slow starter."

Doug won the second hole. "Now I'm on a roll," he told her. But Dara won the third hole. Doug growled.

"Are you one of those guys who can't stand to have a girl beat you?" she asked suspiciously.

"Don't be ridiculous," he said jokingly. "If a girl can beat me, I can take it."

"You goof," she said, handing him the score card. The fourth hole was the most complicated of the entire course. You needed to time your shot so that the arms of a windmill coming down across the pathway would pick the ball up and deposit it on a higher level. There were several players stalled at the hole, and Dara and Doug had to wait their turn.

The thunder was starting up again. A flash of lightning lit the sky. "We're not going to be able to finish this game," Doug said, eyeing the sky. As if in agreement, the couple ahead of them decided to quit. "Just put down that you won, Stevie," the girl said. "You would have anyway."

"Smart," Doug murmured in Dara's ear. "She knows it's not good manners to beat her date."

"Smart nothing," Dara whispered back. "Who wants to win like that?"

"Lots of guys," Doug whispered back through clenched teeth, trying to sound sinister.

"What are you telling me?" Dara giggled. "You want me to throw this game?"

"The thought entered my mind," Doug said, looking over her head and whistling innocently.

"Well, I won't," Dara told him, and laughed.

She stepped up to the tee, watched the windmill go around, waited for the right moment, and tapped the ball. The windmill scooped her ball up and deposited it gently on the second level, barely an inch from the cup. She blew on her nails and stepped back to give Doug his turn.

He placed the ball, studied the mill, then took his shot. The ball rolled onto the arm and was carried up to the second level. It was deposited alongside Dara's, but, for some reason, rolled. It rolled hard and fast enough to drop right into the cup.

"Tied," he announced as he entered their scores and started for the next hole. But the storm came in earnest then. The wind picked up and the rain began. They dropped their clubs in the little start house and ran for Doug's car.

Inside the red Datsun it was dry and cozy. Dara ran her hands through her wet hair and shook the raindrops at Doug. He grabbed her hands and made her stop. They sat that way for a minute, Doug's hands holding both of Dara's prisoner, and Dara felt that funny, fluttering sensation again in her stomach. Doug pulled her gently to him and kissed her lightly.

Dara's eyes closed and stayed that way for a long second. When she opened them, Doug was staring at her. "So listen," he said softly, letting go of her hands, "you want to hang around here until it stops and finish the game?"

"No," she said, and then had to say it again because the first time no sound came from her mouth. She took a deep breath to get her blood to slow down and stop racing around in her body. She could still feel the pressure of his lips on hers.

"Well, then what do you want to do? It's too late to make the movies. I could take you home *really* early and impress your mom."

"No," Dara said emphatically, thinking that the way she felt she didn't ever want to go home. "Why don't we go to the mall and have a sundae?"

"Sounds good," he said, and started the car. Dara leaned over, flicked on the radio, and played with the dial until she found a country-western station. "You listen to that stuff?" Doug asked.

"Not always," Dara said. "It has to be raining, and I have to be driving along Main Street in a red Datsun with someone I like a lot. Country music's not something I share with just anyone."

Doug took one hand off the steering wheel and reached for Dara's. "I like you a lot too," he said. "That month you were away was awful. I wish I could have come up for the final day, but I had a tennis tournament."

"That's okay. I understand," Dara said.

"We have a lot of time to make up for."

Dara leaned her head back against the seat and thought how nice that sounded. "What do you do around here in the summer?" she asked him.

"Oh, we swim at Great Pond, and if nobody's looking we jump off Chicken Rock. We take bike rides out around the reservoir, and hike up Seth Low Mountain. I guess that sounds pretty tame to you."

"Nope," Dara said, smiling at him, "it sounds great."

"Then we do exciting things too," he said. "For instance, this week the seniors are taking their annual unauthorized class trip to Adventureland."

"An amusement park?" Dara said, turning to Doug, her eyes lighting up. "I love roller coasters."

"You do?" Doug glanced over at her. "I knew we were meant for each other. I can never get anyone to go on them with me."

"Now you've got a partner," Dara told him happily. "Kate said she and Pete Hastings are going to that teen disco where they don't serve liquor tomorrow night. How would you feel about going with them?"

"Danceaway? Sure, that's lots of fun," he said happily. "I love to dance."

Dara sat back in her seat and thought, If one more wonderful thing happens, I may explode from sheer joy.

"The Adventureland trip is Thursday," Doug said, turning onto the highway that led to the mall. "We'll be leaving about eight."

"At night?" Dara asked hopefully.

"No," he said, laughing. "In the morning. It's a two-hour trip there, and we want to have the whole day." Then he saw Dara's unhappy expression and asked, "What's the matter?"

"I can't go," she said miserably. "At least I can't go at eight in the morning on Thursday. I have a riding lesson."

"Can't you skip it?"

"No." He looked at her as if he didn't believe her. "I can't," she told him. "I have a competition

coming up soon, and this lesson is very impor-
tant. I need to go over the things I learned at
Langwald's with Mrs. Wiley before I forget them.
My mother would kill me if I missed this lesson."

"Can you change the day?" he asked, searching
for a way to work it out.

Dara shook her head. "The schedule at the
barn is very tight. There's no room to rearrange
lessons. Could we leave later?" she asked him.
That seemed like a reasonable compromise.

"Everybody's leaving at eight, in a convoy. Nuts!"
He took a deep breath and gripped the steering
wheel. "Well," he said philosophically, "I guess it
can't be helped. I know how important your riding is to you. We'll ride those roller coasters
another time."

"Thanks, Doug," she said. "I appreciate your
being so understanding."

"That's okay. Your competitive spirit is one of
the things I like about you."

She started to giggle.

"What's so funny?" he asked.

"Well, actually you owe me a favor."

"I do? For what?"

"For not wanting to stick around and finish the
golf game. Because if we had I'd have beaten
you."

"You're pretty sure of yourself," he said, reaching over to tickle her. She dodged away from his
hand. "You really are competitive, aren't you?"

"In my family you have to be," she said. "Besides, I like winning. It's a nice feeling, something
you can get used to pretty easily."

"I know exactly what you mean," Doug said.

"But"—he leered at her—"tomorrow night at Danceaway may be a different story. Can you tango?"

"Tango?" she asked, horrified. "Of course not. Can you? Can anybody?"

"My dad can," Doug said.

"Well, please don't bring him with you."

"I wasn't about to," Doug said, taking her hand again.

Chapter 3

ON Thursday morning, when Dara woke up, her bedroom was bright with August sunlight. She lay in bed and stared at the window, knowing that all that meant it was going to be brutally hot outside. Her room was cool, and the hum of the air-conditioning system told her that the rest of the house would be just as comfortable. But the ring at Windcroft would be a different story.

She yawned and stretched, and glanced at the clock and tried not to think that right about now she and Doug could have been leaving for Adventureland. "Oh, the sacrifices I make for my sport," she said, yawning again. Tuesday night they'd gone to the disco with Pete and Kate and had a great time, then last night she hadn't heard from him at all, which had surprised her, but she'd see him later. Maybe he'd come over when he got home and they could swim in the pool.

She got out of bed and, wearing only her cotton knit nightshirt that said PHYSICALLY PFHHHT in big red letters across the front, she padded past Matt's closed bedroom door and downstairs. She got herself a glass of orange juice and looked out over the patio to the back lawn. She could see her mother digging in the flower gardens. She opened the door to call good morning.

Her mother waved and said, "It's going to be a scorcher. You're lucky your lesson is early."

"Yeah," Dara murmured, "but I'd be even luckier if I didn't have a lesson at all today." If her mother weren't so adamant about her riding, she might have been tempted to cancel. Not that she didn't love riding—she did. But a whole day with Doug would have been super. She closed the door and fished in the cabinets for some cereal. She sighed and hoped the heat at Windcroft wouldn't be horrendous. Luckily, the ring was mostly shaded until after ten.

Spooning cereal into her mouth, she went over what she wanted to work on with Anne today. In her mind she could hear the creak of the saddle and smell the wonderful smell of the stable; she could almost feel the warm solidity of Arpeggio under her. For many years, riding had been the most important thing. She wondered suddenly if that was still true. Because if it was, then what she did yesterday made no sense. Yesterday she could have worked Arpeggio in the ring by herself, but she hadn't. Instead, she'd taken him on the trails again, and almost felt pleased when she'd told her mother, who hadn't approved.

Dara had the sensation that she was taking her life into her own hands for a change, almost as if she were daring her mother to be mad at her.

"That's pretty dumb, Dara," she said to herself, finishing off the cereal, "considering the fact that your life, at least your riding life, is *not* in your own hands." But there were parts of her life that were her own. Doug, for example. And he was almost as important to her these days as Arpeggio.

She thought about that for a minute and smiled. It was nice having both Doug and Arpeggio. That way, if things went wrong with her riding, she'd still have Doug to take her mind off the problem. And if things went wrong with Doug, she'd have Arpeggio. But things wouldn't go wrong with Doug or Arpeggio. Providing she stopped being a goof-off!

With that in mind, Dara dressed quickly and headed for the stables. She pulled into the driveway at Windcroft and turned off the engine. Almost immediately the car began to heat up. In the ring Dara could see someone riding and for a minute didn't recognize Kate. Then she realized it was because Kate wasn't riding Night Owl, she was riding Northern Spy. Dara walked slowly to the barn, keeping her eye on Kate's lesson. She waved, but Kate was all concentration on her horse and didn't see Dara. The girls used to joke that if a hurricane blew up while Kate was riding, chances are she wouldn't notice.

At the barn door Dara paused, her eyes still on her friend. Something had changed in the way Spy and Kate looked together. Even at this distance she could see how much they had improved as a team since the last time she'd seen Kate ride him.

"Don't they look great?" Jessie said, coming out of the barn to stand with Dara.

"They sure do," Dara agreed. "What happened?
A couple of days seems an awfully short time for
that much improvement. Kate looks as if she's
been riding Spy forever."

"You know Kate. She's a workaholic."

"In all this heat?" Dara said.

"Hey, we peasants have to work for our suc-
cesses," Jessie said teasingly. "We're not all natu-
rals like you and Arpeggio, spending your mornings
in the cool woods." They watched Kate for a few
more minutes, then Jessie said without the least
hint of envy, "It just goes to show you what a
good rider can do with a good horse. I looked like
a rank beginner when I rode Spy."

"You did not," Dara interrupted her. "You looked
great."

"Well, I felt like a rank beginner," Jessie said.
"You were right when you said that Spy wasn't the
horse for me, that he was perfect for Kate. You
think that's why Mrs. Wiley is insisting that Kate
ride Spy, don't you? So Kate'll realize it, too.
That's what you were trying to tell me the other
day at your pool."

Dara nodded.

"I wonder if Kate will ever believe that Night
Owl, dear as he is, isn't the horse she needs," Jessie
asked.

"I don't know," Dara said. "I think it's going to
take someone with a lot more influence than we
have to convince her. Well"—she shook her
head—"I didn't do myself any favors. Kate's going
to be hard to beat on Spy." Dara said it half
jokingly, expecting Jessie to poo-poo the idea,
but Jessie didn't.

"I know," Jessie said. "That made it all the nicer, what you did ... convincing her to ride him." And then seeing the expression on Dara's face, backtracked. "Oh, you won't have any trouble, you and Arpeggio are just as good as Kate and Spy. I mean ..." She stammered, then asked, "Do you have any idea how hard it is to root for two best friends?"

"It's okay, Jessie, I know what you mean," Dara said. "My mother, however, may have a different opinion. I hope she doesn't get to see Kate on Spy anytime soon. By the way, what are you doing here so early?"

"I wanted to get some work done with Time-Out before it gets too hot. You're not the only one sacrificing so that Kate will discover that Spy is the horse for her. After you have your lesson, I have a lesson on Night Owl."

"We really are good friends to go through all this trouble for Kate," Dara said as they walked into the cool, dark barn.

Nodding, Jessie agreed then added, "I wish Kate seemed a little more pleased about it. She's been in a rotten mood for the last two days."

"How is Time-Out?" Dara asked, bringing the conversation around to Jessie's horse.

"She's fine," Jessie said, beaming.

They stopped at the door to Arpeggio's stall. The big gray horse turned around and took a step toward them. Dara reached up to scratch under his forelock. "Hi, big guy," she said. "Ready for a workout?" He made a rumbling sound deep in his chest. "You should be," she said. "You've had it pretty easy these last few days."

"Well, I'm going to muck out some stalls. I'll see you later," Jessie said. But instead of moving away she stayed, looking at Dara.

Dara glanced at her. "What's up?" Jessie moved uncomfortably. "Look," Dara said, "if you think I'm upset about what you said, about Kate being a better rider than I am, I'm not," Dara told her.

"I didn't say that at all," Jessie said.

"Well, whatever it was you did say, forget it."

"I did forget it."

"Then why are you standing there looking at me?"

"I want to ask you something, but I don't know how to put it."

"Ask away," Dara said, slipping on Arpeggio's bridle and clipping the lead line to it to bring him out into the aisle.

"Well ... did you and Doug have a fight?"

"No. Why do you ask?" Dara said as she cross-tied Arpeggio.

"Oh, I knew it was nonsense. I knew if something serious happened between you and Doug, you would have told us."

"So then why the question?"

Jessie sighed. "Last night I went over to the Lickety Split to see Amory." The Lickety Split was the ice cream parlor where Jessie's boyfriend, Amory, worked. "Monica was there. She said she had just seen Gloria Skinner and Doug at the mall, and Gloria told her they were going to Adventureland today."

For a minute Dara couldn't catch her breath. She felt as if she'd been hit. "Are you okay?" Jessie asked, concerned.

"Monica Norton is the eyes and ears of Smithfield," Dara said angrily.

"I know," Jessie said. "And I told her she must have gotten it wrong, and besides, it was none of her business, but she's sure you and Doug have broken up."

"And I bet it made her day," Dara said icily.

"Not really. Monica doesn't care one way or the other, she just likes to gossip. I thought you ought to know what she's saying so you can tell her she's wrong."

"I wouldn't be bothered telling her she's wrong," Dara said. "Besides, she might be right." Dara began brushing Arpeggio's neck.

"Doug did go to Adventureland with Gloria?" Jessie said, amazed.

"He might have. He asked me to go with him but I couldn't because of my lesson. So maybe he did ask Gloria to go with him." She tried to sound nonchalant so that Jessie wouldn't be able to tell how hurt she was. It was very important that Jessie not think it bothered her. She wasn't sure why that was important, but it was.

"It was just a one-time thing, right?" Jessie asked. "Because you couldn't make it."

"Right," Dara said. She continued grooming Arpeggio, keeping her back to Jessie.

"Besides, what difference does it make who he takes to Adventureland, since he asked you first," Jessie said lamely. And when Dara didn't answer, she went on. "Well, I'd better get started on my barn chores. If you're still here when I finish my lesson, maybe we can do something."

"Sure," Dara said, and listened to Jessie walk

off down the aisle. She applied the brush vigorously to Arpeggio. "What difference does it make?"
She repeated Jessie's question in an unbelieving
whisper and then answered it. "It makes a lot of
difference."

"He went to Adventureland with Gloria Skinner!
How could he!" Arpeggio's ears pricked up as if
he were listening to what she was saying. "After
all that stuff he said. He missed me. We were
going to spend the rest of the summer together.
Then he turns around and asks another girl out!"
She bent down to run the brush over Arpeggio's
legs. "That's what I get for trusting him, for thinking he's so considerate!" Arpeggio shook his head
up and down as if he were in total agreement
with her.

Dara put the brush away and took the hoof
pick. Lifting Arpeggio's feet one at a time, she
carefully cleaned away the bedding and dirt caught
in the soft part of his hoof. "How could he?" she
asked again softly, and then her hurt turned to
anger. "If he wants to play games, fine and dandy.
I can play them, too."

Arpeggio stood staring at her, his big, intelligent
eyes looking anxious.

"I'm not mad at you, Arpeggio. You wouldn't do
that to me, would you? You'd never turn on me
like that." She placed her cheek against the big
gray's neck for a minute and told herself she most
definitely did *not* feel like crying and those funny
wet things on her cheeks were not tears. She was
Dara "the cool" Cooper. That was the nickname
Kate had given her. And things like this did not
happen to her. She blinked several times, and her

eyes cleared. Then without another word she saddled and bridled Arpeggio and led him out into
the hot sun.

Kate was coming toward the barn, riding Spy
with a loose rein. Over his chest his chestnut
coat looked black from sweat. Kate looked as
warm as he did, her face flushed and shiny with
perspiration. "It's going to take me a year to cool
him down," she said.

"Yeah," Dara agreed, trying to make her voice
sympathetic, but failing. The word came out cold
and curt. Kate gave her a funny look, but Dara
didn't feel like explaining herself and continued
up toward the ring.

On the shady side of the ring, Anne Wiley,
Kate's mother, leaned against the rails, drinking a
can of seltzer. "Hi," she called to Dara.

Dara waved back. She liked Anne Wiley a lot.
She was an excellent coach. Maybe she wasn't
famous like the man who coached Dara in Pennsylvania, but she knew just as much. And she was
nicer. She was really interested in Dara and Arpeggio. The coach in Pennsylvania had been, too,
but for a different reason. He'd been interested
because she was so good and Arpeggio was so
special. If she'd been one of the run-of-the-mill
riders, he wouldn't have paid any attention to her
at all.

But Mrs. Wiley wasn't like that. She gave Jessie,
who wasn't competing at the same level as Kate
and Dara, just as much attention as she did Dara,
and she gave Dara just as much attention as she
did her own daughter.

"How's your leg this morning?" Dara asked,

forcing a smile and trying to put the news about Doug and Gloria behind her.

"Feeling better and better," Anne said. She'd had surgery on her knee this past spring to repair an old jumping injury, and had just recently started getting around without crutches. "I'll let you in on a secret. I'm starting Jonathan over cavalletti." Jonathan was Mrs. Wiley's horse.

"You're training him to jump?" Dara asked excitedly. "You're going to try jumping again?"

"I'm going to try," Anne said. "If Jonathan ever gets his courage up. He used to jump, but it's been so long, he's forgotten how. And I don't want to get on a horse that's going to refuse. My own jumping courage is rather shaky, and I need a horse that will help me."

"I'll be glad to school Jonathan if you like."

"Thanks, honey. I'll keep that in mind, but you have your hands full with this guy." Anne gestured toward Arpeggio.

"Kate looked awfully good on Spy." Dara stopped just inside the ring to adjust her stirrups again.

Mrs. Wiley finished the last of her seltzer and dropped the can in a plastic bag she had hung from one of the posts. "I agree. Kate looks very good. She's been working like a demon these last few days. She and Spy want to get their act together before they take it on the road. I understand you did a little pushing to get Kate up on Spy's back."

"A little," Dara said. "Jessie and I figured it out a while back. Now we understand that Mr. Yon wanted Kate to have Spy, that's why he could never find anyone good enough to buy him. Then

Kate messed his plans all up by arranging for Jessie to ride him."

"Well, you two are pretty sharp." Mrs. Wiley laughed. "Kate did mess up a lot of carefully laid plans. Well, I hope riding Spy at Waterfall Farm will help her realize that much as she loves Night Owl, he can't do what she wants him to do." Then she paused. "Providing what she wants him to do is take her to the Olympics. But that's a decision she'll have to make. I can advise, but I certainly can't make her mind up for her." Mrs. Wiley paused for a minute and looked at Dara. "Are you all right? You look a little . . . funny."

"I'm fine," Dara said quickly.

"Okay, then let's get going before the sun clears those trees. Circle him at the trot. Keep it slow. Get a good beat going." Dara turned Arpeggio to the right and applied her leg to him, asking him to pick up an easy trot. "That's it," Anne said, "one-two, one-two. Your right hand is dropping, Dara, keep it up."

Dara posted as the big gray moved under her. She lost herself briefly in the rhythm of riding, and the thought of how wonderful her horse was. And how wonderful it was to do something well. She loved the confidence she felt when she rode. In the past it had made all her other problems fade away, and it would now, too. It drove home what her mother had been telling her for a long time. "First your riding, then everything else."

"You're losing him, Dara, watch his shoulders on the corners." Anne's voice startled Dara, and she brought her attention back to Arpeggio. "Keep him coming forward. That's it, but don't let him rush the corners."

Dara hadn't realized that's what Arpeggio was doing. She stopped posting and did a sitting trot so she would have more contact with the saddle and be more aware of what the horse was doing. A fine mist of perspiration formed on her forehead. Even with the ring still shaded, it was hot. If the fates were fair, the air-conditioning in Doug's car would have broken down and he and Gloria would be sweating, too. She hoped all of Gloria's mascara was running down her cheeks. All the unhappiness she had felt at the news of Gloria and Doug came back to her with a rush.

"Dara, you're letting him take control. Make him wait for you. Your left hand is dropping again. Move your thumb and bend your elbow."

Dara looked down at her hands. What was Anne talking about? Her thumb was right where it should be.

"What's with Arpeggio today?" Anne asked. "He's flattened out. Get him rounded up. Maybe I'm just not used to seeing him after Spy," Anne offered. "Arpeggio always looked so good against Night Owl. Keep him coming forward. There, that's better. Can you feel the difference?"

Dara nodded, but the truth was she couldn't. She couldn't feel much of anything except a rush of anger every time she thought of Doug.

"Let's try a canter," Anne called. "Good, he picked that up nicely. That's it, keep him coming." Anne watched them make a complete circle of the ring, then said, "I'm going to have to give you some exercises to tuck his hindquarters a little, get him driving from underneath."

Was that what she meant by rounding him up, Dara wondered. That was one of the things about

Spy that made him so beautiful to watch. His hindquarters were beautifully muscled, and he used them to good advantage. He kept his rear legs under him, driving from behind so that the picture he showed was of a well-collected horse . . . a nice, round picture.

That was one of the things Tommy Langwald liked best about Arpeggio. What was Anne Wiley trying to tell her? Dara forced herself to pay attention to what she was doing, and she succeeded for almost a full minute before Doug and Gloria took over again. She had a picture of them in the roller coaster, Gloria hanging on to Doug for all she was worth.

"He's diving, Dara, you're letting him hang on the bit." Anne's voice brought her back again. "Make him support his own weight."

Dara had been pulling on the reins, balancing the weight of Arpeggio's head on the bit, thinking of Doug, balancing the weight of Gloria, hanging on his arm. She lessened the tension immediately, and Arpeggio increased his pace.

"If you're going to loosen the rein, you have to sit back and control him with your legs and seat," Anne called.

"I know," Dara shot back sharply. "I know. Give me a chance."

"Don't go forward with him when he speeds up," Anne said.

"I know that, too," Dara said angrily. "That's practically the first thing I learned." She could feel Anne's eyes on her but she refused to meet them.

"But you're not controlling him, Dara. I wouldn't be doing my job if I didn't point it out."

Grimly, Dara adjusted her position again, and this time Arpeggio came to a faltering halt and then when she applied her leg to him took off at a trot instead of the canter they had been doing. "What's the matter with him?" she asked in exasperation.

"Nothing," Anne said. "Let him walk a minute and you try to calm down. This heat has probably gotten to you."

"He's not listening to me," Dara said as she walked Arpeggio around the ring on a loose rein.

"You're not telling him much," Anne said.

"What's that mean?"

"Well, your form's a little sloppy," Anne said, trying to be kind. "You're not as straight and alert as you usually are. I didn't think you looked well when you came into the ring. I don't know, you're kind of slouching, the line from the bit to your elbow is wrong, and you're leaning forward too much. Kate used to do that, but—"

"I'm not sick and I'm riding the same way I always have," Dara interrupted.

"You're not, honey, or you wouldn't be having trouble. It's nothing to get upset over. Riders go through these things all the time. If you learned to ride perfectly and then never changed, you wouldn't have any use for a coach. Here, have a cold drink, maybe that'll fix you up."

"No, thanks," Dara said. "Could we just keep going?"

They went through the exercises again, and this time Anne said very little. Then she stopped Dara and walked into the center of the ring to stand next to her. "I know you're kind of touchy today, but I need to ask you something. Did Tommy say anything to you about getting Arpeggio's rear end underneath him more? Did he give you any exercises to do?"

"No. He didn't say anything to me at all about that. Why?"

"I don't know," Anne said. "I'm not sure if Arpeggio's suddenly taken to being lazy, or he can tell that you're not really paying attention, but he's pulling himself along instead of pushing off with his hindquarters. Maybe it's just that the heat's got him, too."

Dara stared at Anne and felt a rush of anger that took in the whole world. "I am paying attention," she said grimly. "I'm riding him the way I've always ridden him. Maybe seeing Kate on Spy has made every other horse and rider look terrible to you."

"Dara," Anne said, surprised.

"I rode for an entire month at Langwald's and he didn't complain about the way I rode or the way Arpeggio looked."

"Not at all?" Anne said.

"Not at all," Dara told her.

"Then you didn't get your money's worth," Anne said.

The tears that had pricked Dara's eyes earlier in the barn were back. She held her lids rigidly open so they wouldn't spill down her cheeks and embarrass her in front of Anne. "Mrs. Wiley," she said with as much control as she could muster, "you are right, I'm not feeling well. I'd just as soon cancel this lesson." And before Anne could say a word, Dara left the ring.

Chapter 4

JESSIE was just about to tack up Night Owl when Dara came back into the barn. "Is an hour up already?" Jessie asked, looking quickly at her watch.

"No," Dara said. "I didn't finish my lesson."

"Why not?"

"Because," Dara said, and slipped Arpeggio's saddle off.

"Do you want to get by us and put him in his stall?" Jessie asked, pushing against Night Owl's haunches to move him over.

"No, I have to cool him down. I'll see you later."

"Dara?" Jessie called. "Are you upset about Doug?"

"Of course not."

"Because Monica probably had things all screwy. Don't sit around all day and stew over it," Jessie warned, concern in her voice.

"I'm not stewing over anything," Dara said, work-

44

ing hard to keep her voice normal. If there was one thing she didn't want, it was people feeling sorry for her. "Why don't you come over this afternoon and we can swim," she said, putting a bright smile on her face, which she figured looked pretty silly with the unhappiness in her eyes.

"I can't," Jessie told her. "I promised Sarah I'd bring her back to the barn. She's going to help me clean some tack and then I promised her a ride on Time-Out." Sarah was Jessie's younger sister. "Why don't you come over, too?"

Cleaning tack was not the way Dara thought she'd be spending the afternoon. If she refused, Jessie would go on thinking it was because she was so upset with Doug, no matter what Dara said, so she agreed.

"Okay," Dara told her. "I'll see you here after lunch." She took Arpeggio back outside, sponged him off, and walked him around in front of the barn. She kept her eyes on the ground right in front of her, afraid that if she looked up she'd find Anne Wiley watching her. But she needn't have worried. The ring was empty.

When Arpeggio was finally cool enough to put back in his stall, Dara left him and started quickly for home.

The house was wonderfully chilly, almost cold enough to need a sweater. Matt was lying on the couch in the den reading a science fiction novel. "Where's Mom?" Dara asked.

"She's gone to the nursery to get some special kind of flowers. She was all excited when she found out that they had whatever it was she wanted. Has she joined the garden club here yet?"

Dara shook her head. "I'm not sure they have one in Smithfield."

"If they don't, Mom'll start one." Matt stuck his finger in his book for a marker and asked, "What does she do here all day? She doesn't seem to have the projects and committee stuff she used to have in Lancaster."

"I'm not sure what she does," Dara said, shrugging.

"And where've you been?" Matt asked.

"Riding."

"Mad dogs and horseback riders go out in the eight o'clock sun," he said, paraphrasing the song. "But smart Yalies stay in the house and read."

"I'm going to take a shower," she said, refusing to comment on his remark.

In a few minutes she was back downstairs, dressed in a pair of yellow shorts and a yellow-and-white tank top. "Do you want a snack?" she asked.

"Sure." Matt put his book down and followed her into the kitchen. "Yogurt, cottage cheese, hard-boiled eggs," he said, scanning the contents of the refrigerator. "Don't you guys stock any real food?"

Dara opened a cupboard door and handed him some chunky peanut butter and a jar of grape jelly.

"Ambrosia," he sighed.

They sat at the table and slathered slices of bread with the peanut butter and jelly, and washed the sandwiches down with cold milk. "So," Matt said after swallowing half his sandwich, "you really like it here, don't you?"

Dara looked at him and then out the window. "Yeah," she said.

"But then, you'd get along anyplace. I wonder if you know how lucky you are?"

"It would be hard for me not to know," Dara said. "People tell me all the time."

Matt laughed, and then said, "But in your case it's true. Things fall right in your lap."

And sometimes, Dara thought, when they land, they hurt. "How do *you* like it here?" she asked.

"I guess it's nice. I probably would have liked going to high school here. But to be honest with you, I'm bored stiff. I don't know a soul."

"That must be hard," Dara agreed. "I'm going to meet Jessie at the stable this afternoon. Want to come?"

"Jessie's the real pretty one with brown hair? What are you going to do there?"

"We're going to clean tack and then give her little sister a riding lesson. I could lead you around on Arpeggio," Dara offered with a smile.

"Not exactly my idea of excitement," Matt said. "Besides, no insult intended, but you guys are a little young for me." He dipped his knife into the peanut butter and scooped up a last mouthful. "Hey, Dara, old buddy, old chum, would you do me a favor?"

"Probably not," Dara said warily. Most of Matt's favors involved Dara running interference between Matt and their parents.

"It's no big deal. All I want you to do is find a way to mention to Mom how hard it is on me here, not having any friends and stuff, and how it would be nice if I could spend the rest of the summer with my friends."

Dara studied him. "You want to go back to Lancaster for the summer?"

"No. I didn't like it there any more than you did. I want to use the beach house in Rhode Island. I met this girl in school, and she's working as a waitress up there. I'd like to spend a little time with her."

"A waitress?" Dara said. "I thought you told Mom you were dating her sorority sister's daughter?"

"I said I'd called her sorority sister's daughter," Matt corrected Dara. "I didn't say I'd dated her."

"Mom's going to be disappointed," Dara said.

"As long as you're dating Mr. Popularity of Smithfield she won't worry too much about me. So will you work it into the conversation?"

"Why don't you just ask her yourself?"

"You know I'm not in her good graces at the moment because of my marks."

Dara shrugged, then gave in. "All right, I'll see what I can do."

"What's wrong with you?" Matt asked after they'd sat for a few silent minutes. "You're usually bubbling all over the place."

"I have not had my best day of all times," Dara said.

"Didn't the riding go well?"

"Not very."

"One bad lesson has you this depressed?"

"I'm not depressed, I'm angry. Besides, the lesson wasn't bad. Mrs. Wiley was in some kind of funny mood. But the big news is that Mr. Popularity is dating someone else." She told him about the trip to Adventureland and Monica's story.

"That's not exactly dating someone else," Matt said. "A group trip to an amusement park isn't exactly a commitment for life. Couldn't you have missed just one lesson to go with him?"

She stared at him. "Canceling a lesson is a decision I can't make by myself."

"Mom?" he asked, and Dara nodded. "So, just tell her you're canceling. She'll get mad, but it blows over."

"This lesson was important. It was the first lesson I had with Anne after spending a month at the clinic. We were supposed to go over all the stuff I learned there." She rested her chin on her hand and looked out the window, thinking about her lesson and how poorly it went.

"And if you didn't do that you might miss a couple of blue ribbons," Matt said with a touch of sarcasm.

"You know," Dara said with the bite of anger in her words, "I don't have it as easy as you think I do. When Mom bought me Arpeggio, it was with the agreement that I could keep him as long as I stayed ahead of everyone else. That means blue ribbons. If I don't get enough of them, if I start slipping, then Arpeggio goes."

"You're kidding?" Matt said. "Why'd you go along with that?"

"Because I wanted Arpeggio so badly," Dara said, her voice deep with emotion. She remembered as if it were yesterday the first time she'd laid eyes on the big gray. He was without a doubt the most beautiful horse Dara had ever seen. And then the first time she'd ridden him was like a dream. He seemed to know what she wanted him to do before she did. Dara felt as if they were one being.

Matt looked at his sister, and she could see the caring in his eyes. "Does Doug know that? About Arpeggio?" he asked.

"No."

"If I were you, I'd call him and get it straightened out. He probably thinks you just like riding better than you like him. No guy wants to play second fiddle to a horse. Besides, maybe the whole thing's a lie anyway. After all, you got the story secondhand."

"No," Dara said, breaking out of her mood and carrying her dishes to the sink. "If he cared enough about me, he'd have done things differently, or at least told me he was going to ask Gloria. Besides, Monica's story has the ring of truth to it. Doug and Gloria went out a couple of times before he started dating me."

"Well, maybe he wants to date both of you."

"Well, maybe he does, but I don't. Let's drop the subject. You sure you don't want to come to the stable?"

"I've never been so positive about anything in my life."

"See you later, then," Dara said.

As usual, the barn was cool. The old oaks and maples that ringed it kept most of it shaded. Dara sat on her tack box, her long legs folded under her, a bridle stretched across her lap. She was cleaning the leather with an oil soap solution, rubbing back and forth to loosen the grime. Jessie gave Sarah a stirrup and a can of metal cleaner and told her to start polishing. Sarah set to work with a determined face, glancing now and then at Jessie and Dara. "I'm working harder than you are," she said proudly.

"You sure are," Jessie said. "You're a good worker."

"What would you do if Amory asked another girl out?" Dara asked Jessie.

"I thought you weren't upset about it."

"I'm not," Dara said, keeping her voice level. "I'm just curious."

"Oh, Dara, you can't compare people. Amory and I are completely different from Doug and you. In the first place, I think Doug likes you more than Amory likes me. Well, maybe not more," she amended, "but in a different way. Amory and I are friends. So if he really wanted to go someplace and I couldn't go with him and he asked someone else, I don't think I'd get that upset. And, if it was *really* important to him for me to go, too, I'd probably have cancelled my lesson and gone with him."

Dara dipped her cloth into the cleaning solution, rinsed it out, and rubbed it again over the bridle. "He didn't cancel his tennis match to come up to Langwald's to see me."

"That was totally different," Jessie said, standing up to take down a pair of braided reins from the hook. "If you were in a competition, then I could see not being able to go. But it was just a lesson."

"And for all the good it did me, I *could* have skipped it. How was *your* lesson with Mrs. Wiley?"

"Pretty good. I'm not as sure on Night Owl as Kate is, so I need a lot of correction." Jessie wet her own rag and pulled the reins through it.

"Did Mrs. Wiley tell you to watch the way Kate rides so you can improve?"

"No," Jessie said, and looked at Dara. "That was a strange question."

"Jessie, how's this?" Sarah asked, holding up the stirrup.

"Great," Jessie said. "Just a little more underneath."

Jessie sighed and examined the reins she held. "I hope things even out soon because I'm getting pretty tired of everybody being uptight. Maybe Mrs. Wiley wasn't her old self because she's trying to get Jonathan to jump again and he's not being cooperative. He keeps refusing even the smallest jumps. And Kate is in knots trying to get Spy ready for Waterfall and you're all upset because of Doug...."

"I'm not upset," Dara said, turning her intense blue eyes on Jessie.

"Sure," Jessie said, and looked away.

Dara hung up her bridle and brought down her reins. "What's Kate so uptight about? I saw her lesson. I thought she looked great."

"I did, too, but you know Kate. She doesn't think she looked great."

"I hope she doesn't turn into one of these slit-your-throat competitors," Dara said, rubbing harder than was necessary at her reins.

"Kate?" Jessie said, amazed.

"Don't sound surprised. I've seen it happen before. You should have been around the barn in Concordia on an event day. The tension was so thick you could cut it with a knife. And the parents were worse than the riders. When you went into the ring you had the feeling that even though everyone was saying good luck they really hoped you'd fall off your horse!"

"And you think it'll get that way between you and Kate?"

"Maybe," Dara said.

"Dara, you've been out in the sun too long," Jessie said angrily.

"Well, I noticed a definite change in the way Mrs. Wiley was schooling me today. She kept nagging at me about things."

"So?"

"So she never used to do that. Today she kept saying that after watching Spy go, Arpeggio didn't look too good."

"Mrs. Wiley would never say a thing like that," Jessie said, shocked.

"Well, she did," Dara insisted.

"Are you sure you weren't just hearing things because you were all riled up about Doug?"

"For the millionth time, I am not riled up about Doug! And I don't hear things," Dara almost screamed.

"You heard me say some things that I never said," Jessie muttered. "Is that why your lesson ended so early?" she asked, studying Dara.

"I guess I was kind of rude to her," Dara said, quieting down. "But I've just come back from four weeks of intensive training with one of the best horsemen in the country, and he didn't find half as much to complain about as Mrs. Wiley did. He didn't pick my skills apart."

"You think Mrs. Wiley was picking on you?" Jessie asked.

"Well, she sure didn't complain about much in Kate's lesson."

"How do you know? You weren't at it. Besides, Mrs. Wiley doesn't play favorites, if that's what you're hinting at," Jessie said. "And if you were rude to her, you owe her an apology. You do, Dara," Jessie insisted when Dara remained silent.

Dara sighed and looked over Sarah's bent head to the fields outside the barn. Maybe Jessie was right. Maybe the heat had gotten to her. She hoped that's all it was, because she didn't like the way she felt inside. All of a sudden everything she loved about Smithfield had changed overnight. "I guess you're right," she said. "I'll call her tomorrow. Are you going out with Amory tonight?" Jessie shook her head. "Want to go to a movie?"

"Sure," Jessie said. "I'll call Kate and set it up."

Sarah was back standing in front of Jessie with a sparkling stirrup in her hand. "Perfect," Jessie said, and handed her the other one.

"After this can I ride Time-Out?"

"Sure," Jessie said.

Sighing, Dara hung her reins back up. "I'm going to head home," she said. "I don't really feel like doing this. Besides, it's dumb not to be in a pool in this weather. Why don't you and Sarah come swimming?"

Sarah's eyes lit up. "Oh, goodie, Jessie, let's, please?" And then her expression changed and she looked at Jessie. "But after I ride Time-Out."

Even Dara, for all her moodiness, had to laugh. "Come over whenever you want to," she said. "I'll be there all afternoon." She stood up and started for the door.

"It might not be a bad idea for both of us to watch the way Kate rides," Jessie said quietly. "Maybe, if Mrs. Wiley suggested it, she was trying to be helpful." Dara stopped halfway out the door and stared at Jessie. "Maybe Kate will tell you this herself. I sort of found out by accident," Jessie said. "But, on the last day of camp, Tommy Langwald called Kate into his office and told her that she was one of the best riders to come through his clinics in a long time."

Dara stared at Jessie. "Tommy Langwald told Kate that?"

Jessie nodded, the look in her eyes changing as she went from being happy for Kate to being upset for Dara. Dara, seeing the problem Jessie was having, pulled herself together. "That's wonderful," she said, forcing some warmth into her voice, and was rewarded to see Jessie look relieved.

"In that case, maybe Mrs. Wiley was right," Dara said, and waved airily. "See you when I see you," she said, and continued out of the barn. In the driveway she fumbled the key into the lock, then slipped into her car. That's what Tommy had told Kate that last day at the clinic. But why had she come out of his office looking so upset?

It was hot as an oven in the little car. Dara started the motor and turned the air-conditioner on full blast. Tommy Langwald had gone out of his way to tell Kate how good she was and never said a word to Dara? Dara sighed and hung her head over the steering wheel. If her mother found out about this, Dara would never hear the end of it.

Chapter 5

"WELL," Jessie said, settling into a booth at the Lickety Split and looking at her watch, "it's still only ten o'clock."

"How come we went to the early show?" Kate asked.

"Because I have to get up early," Dara fibbed. The real reason that she couldn't bear to go to the later show was that the kids who had dates went then, and she didn't want anyone to see her dateless. The story about Doug and Gloria was probably all over town by now.

"What are you so touchy about?" Kate asked her.

"Nothing," Dara fibbed again.

"I think you should tell her," Jessie said.

"Tell me what?" Kate asked.

"Well, I guess now I'll have to." Dara gave Jessie a stern look and told Kate about Doug and Gloria. "See," Dara said to Jessie. "That's exactly what I didn't want."

56

"What?" Jessie said, looking from Kate to Dara in confusion.

"That look," Dara said. "That I-feel-sorry-for-you look that Kate just gave me."

"Did I do that?" Kate asked Jessie.

"Yes," Dara said. "And everyone else in town who knows is going to look at me the same way. I hate it when people think they have to feel sorry for me."

"Well, count me out of that group," Kate said. "I certainly don't feel sorry for you." Dara heard an edge to her voice. "How come you told Jessie about Doug and didn't tell me?"

"*I* didn't tell Jessie," Kate said. "She told me. Besides, you've got some secrets, too."

"What'll it be, girls?" A waitress stood at the table, pad in hand.

"Where's Amory tonight?" Kate asked Jessie. Amory usually worked at the ice cream parlor.

"He's got the night off. He went to the jai alai game in Hartford."

The girls ordered and the waitress left to fix their sundaes.

"I saw you on Spy today," Dara said to Kate, making an effort to get the evening back on friendly ground. "You looked very good."

It was an opening if Kate wanted to tell her about Tommy Langwald's compliment, but all Kate said was "Thanks," and Dara thought even that one word was rather cool.

"How did you make out on Night Owl?" Kate asked Jessie.

"Fine," Jessie said. "'We're not going to be any

competition for you or Dara, but we won't make fools of ourselves."

"You've got too much going for you to make a fool of yourself," Kate said, then added under her breath, "unlike someone else I know."

Dara leaned toward Kate and asked, "What is it with you tonight? Are you mad at me or something?"

"Yeah," Kate said, looking Dara straight in the eye. "I am. My mom is killing herself to get us ready for that competition at Waterfall Farm. She hasn't been off her crutches that long, and her leg still bothers her when she's on it too much. She's trying to get back into jumping herself, and her horse is not cooperating, but she pushes all she can to help us."

Dara looked at her uncomfortably. Mrs. Wiley must have told Kate how Dara had acted in the ring today. It surprised her a little. She hadn't thought Mrs. Wiley would tell tales, but then, Kate *was* her daughter. "I guess I do owe your mother an apology," Dara said. "I'm going to call her tomorrow."

"Don't you think it would be more appropriate if your mother called and apologized?"

"My mother?" Dara asked blankly. "What does my mother have to do with this?"

"Your mother called my mom this afternoon and she was very upset. She said that she'd seen part of your lesson this morning and that your riding was slipping. That since you've been here in Smithfield, she could see that your skills were going downhill. That even the month with Langwald hadn't brought you back to where you were when you were taking lessons with the king of eventing back in Pennsylvania!"

"My mom did that?" Dara asked, shocked.

"Your mom did that," Kate answered sharply.

"I didn't even know she was at my lesson."

"Well, she was." Kate sat glaring at Dara with a what-are-you-going-to-do-about-it look in her eyes. Dara turned away.

"Listen, guys," Jessie said nervously. "Let's calm down."

"That's swell," Dara said, glancing at Jessie. "First Langwald thinks my riding is mediocre, then my mother does."

"Langwald never said your riding was mediocre," Jessie said in exasperation. "Why are you jumping to conclusions?"

"He also never called me into his office and said I was the best rider he'd seen in a long time."

Kate stared at Dara for a minute and then turned on Jessie. "You told her."

"Well," Jessie said uncomfortably.

"Why didn't you want me to know?" Dara demanded.

"Because, I ... what difference does it make? I just didn't." Kate's voice was riding. "I didn't want Jessie to know either, it just slipped out."

"Guys," Jessie wailed, "stop it."

"Look, Cooper," Kate said, pushing her ice cream away and standing up. "What Langwald said to me has nothing to do with what your mother said to my mother. Your mother didn't think we were good enough for you the first time she came out to the stable. Maybe you'd better look for someplace better." She turned and walked away. She was halfway to the door before she turned back, "What were *you* going to apologize to my mom for?" she asked, glaring at Dara.

"Never mind." Dara glared back.

"Well, if you've been insulting her, too, you darned well better apologize." Then she turned quickly and ran out the door.

"Kate," Jessie called, getting up, too.

"Go ahead, go after her," Dara said. "I know you think she's right."

"She is right about you apologizing, Dara," Jessie said, sitting at the edge of her seat. "Mrs. Wiley is a great coach, and if she told you something, I know it's for your own good, even if you don't want to hear it." She looked sorrowfully out the door where Kate had disappeared. "Now, how is she going to get home?" she asked.

"She knows where the car is," Dara said.

"Forget that," Jessie told her. "She'll never show up at the car. She's got just as much pride as you do. Well, I'm certainly not in the mood for this," Jessie said, stirring her spoon around in her whipped cream.

"Me neither. Let's go."

Jessie had been right, there was no sign of Kate at the car. The ride back to Smithfield was silent except for the radio. Jessie said no more than a curt good-night when Dara pulled into her drive. Halfway to her own house, Dara changed her mind and drove around aimlessly. She made several turns and found herself at Windwing Road. That must be where the lake was, the lake that Doug had said they'd be spending so much time at. She turned down the rutted dirt road and

parked the car. Ahead of her the lake shimmered
in the moonlight.

She stared out over it and wondered if Doug
was home yet. "What difference does it make,"
she told herself angrily. She had no intention of
seeing him again. As a matter of fact, there was a
good possibility that for the rest of the summer
she wouldn't see anyone at all, since Jessie and
Kate were both mad at her.

She ran her finger along the steering wheel,
and for some reason in her mind's eye she pic-
tured Kate on Northern Spy. They were so graceful together, so right. She saw people congratulating
Kate on her riding and she saw the same people
trying to find something nice to say to her ...
something that wouldn't hurt her feelings but that
would still be true. Things like "You're such a
competent rider" and "What a fine horse he is."
She'd said the same things herself to other riders
at other competitions, all the while thinking how
bad they must feel because they hadn't won.

She didn't begrudge Kate and Spy their future
triumphs, although Dara doubted her mother would
feel the same way. But what would she do if she
didn't win anymore and lost Arpeggio? She didn't
know how to be anyone but a winner or anyplace
but on top. And she didn't know how to fix things
when they went wrong. She'd had no practice at
it.

And she didn't want people's sympathy, not
about Arpeggio and not about Doug, and not about
the fact that she'd just alienated the two best
friends she'd ever had. What *do* you want, Dara?
The question buzzed around in her brain. "I

want things to be the way they were," she said. But that was like wanting snow in July.

Wearily, she started the car and drove home. The lights were on in the house and Dara walked in to find her mother in the kitchen. Dara had the impulse to run to her and put her arms around her mom and tell her what a lousy day she'd had, but she didn't. She used to be able to do that, but somehow over the last few years they'd stopped hugging. Instead, Dara stood quietly in the doorway.

"How was the movie?" Mrs. Cooper asked.

"The movie?" Dara said dumbly. So much had happened since the movie she'd almost forgotten they'd seen one. "It was okay. How come you didn't tell me you'd seen my lesson?"

"There wasn't much to tell, was there? That was the poorest I've ever seen you ride."

"But you told Mrs. Wiley," Dara said.

"That's right, I did. I've hired her to keep your riding up to competition levels, and she's not doing that."

"I haven't ridden, really ridden, since horse camp, Mom," Dara said. "And it was blistering hot today. I just need some time to get back into the swing of things."

"You don't have that much time. Waterfall is right around the corner. Besides, you just spent a month in Vermont with that Langwald man. Is it possible you lost everything he taught you in less than a week? If that's the case, either I just threw a lot of money away or you're getting lazy. You'd better start applying yourself, young lady."

"I'm doing the best I can," Dara said, and even as she said them the words sounded familiar.

Those were the words Matthew used almost every time he got into a discussion with their parents about his schoolwork.

"Are you?" her mother asked in a doubtful tone. And those words were just as familiar. Those were the same words and tone her parents used to answer Matt.

Dara turned and fled, taking the stairs to her bedroom two at a time. In her room she threw herself onto her bed without bothering to turn on the lights.

How could life go from perfect to awful in so short a time? She turned over on her back and stared at the dark ceiling. Things had gotten so mixed up, there didn't seem to be any way to straighten them out. Her riding, which once had brought her only happiness, now was causing her all kinds of trouble. She felt a little sick to her stomach. The rest of the summer stretched in front of her endlessly, no girlfriends, no boyfriends, and her riding on the skids.

Thank heaven Matt was home. At least they'd have each other. They could hole up here at the house like two hermits. How she would face everyone when school started again was another story, but she wasn't going to think about that now. But Monica's smiling face rose up to taunt her.

She sat up on the edge of her bed and stared into the darkness. Her mother had wanted to send her to a private school when her father had been transferred. She and Dara had even looked at some, but none of the ones Mrs. Cooper approved of had boarding facilities for a horse. If things were really bad when she got back to school, maybe she could transfer. And if her riding didn't improve and her mother kept to her promise, boarding facilities for a horse wouldn't matter, Arpeggio would be gone anyway.

The telephone rang, and Dara glanced quickly at her clock radio. A wild hope that it might be Doug raced through her. Maybe he could explain why he'd taken Gloria to Adventureland without saying a word to Dara about his intentions. But it was after eleven; he wouldn't call her that late. She heard her father answer it and then heard his footsteps on the stairs. He tapped at her door and opened it. "Dara, it's Mrs. Wiley. She wants to talk to you."

Dara sighed and let her head hang. "Dad, could you tell her I'm sleeping?"

Her father studied her for a minute. "I don't like telling her lies," he said.

"Then just tell her I'm in bed. That's the truth." She lay back down and pulled the sheet up over her. She heard the door close and her father's steps as he went back down the stairs. In a short time he returned. "Mrs. Wiley says it's very important that she talk to you. She wants you to come to the farm tomorrow morning at nine."

"Did you say I'd go?" Dara asked.

"Yes, of course," Mr. Cooper said. "And if that wasn't right, you should have talked to her yourself. Good night." He closed the door firmly behind him.

Maybe it was a good thing. She'd go to the farm, apologize to Mrs. Wiley, and then start looking for another place to ride for whatever time she had left with Arpeggio. There must be a coach in the area that didn't know the Wileys. She'd pretend Windcroft and Doug and her friends had never happened. She was used to depending on no one but herself. She had spent years at Concordia perfecting that ability.

Chapter 6

MATT had asked to borrow Dara's car, and drove Dara to the Wileys' house the next morning, promising to be back in two hours. Walking toward the house, Dara noticed that Jessie's bike was leaning against the oak tree in front. Dara wasn't sure whether she was relieved or upset that Jessie would be there, too. She forced herself up the path to the back door, drew a deep breath, and knocked. "Come in," Anne Wiley called from the kitchen.

Kate was standing at the sink washing dishes, Jessie was sitting at the table, and Mrs. Wiley was pouring lemonade into three glasses. She smiled at Dara and offered her one of the glasses.

"Thanks," Dara said, and remained standing awkwardly where she was. There was an uneasy quiet.

"Okay, girls," Mrs. Wiley said. "I don't know what's going on, but whatever it is, I want to see it end here and now."

"I don't know what you expect Jessie and *me* to do," Kate said, her back still toward the rest of them. It was obvious from her tone that a discussion had been going on before Dara got there.

"Mrs. Wiley," Dara said, ignoring Kate's words. "I want to apologize to you for being rude. And I want to apologize for my mother. She shouldn't have called you."

Mrs. Wiley smiled at Dara. "These things happen," she said. "It's really nothing to get this upset about. I personally think August is responsible for more unhappy encounters than any other month in the year. All this heat and humidity is making everybody disagreeable. Why don't we just forget about it?"

"I agree," Jessie said, but she was the only one who answered.

"We can reschedule your lesson, Dara, if you like."

"No," Dara said, staring miserably at Kate's back. "I'm considering moving to another stable." Even as she said the words she wished she could call them back. It was all so stupid. She wasn't considering that at all. Those dumb things she had thought about last night were just that: *dumb*. She didn't want to move to another stable, she didn't want to go to a private school. She wanted things to be the way they were.

"Well, we can talk about it later," Mrs. Wiley said softly, and Dara could see the regret in her eyes. "But where you have your horse or where you train shouldn't affect the friendship you girls have. I think the three of you ought to take the horses out on the trails and do something fun today, while it's still cool enough to do anything at all, and put all this silly bickering behind you."

"Good," Jessie said, finishing off her drink and standing up. "I'm all for that."

"You go ahead," Kate said. She still hadn't turned around.

"Kate Wiley," Mrs. Wiley said with a hint of exasperation in her voice. "I want you out on the trails."

"Spy could probably use the exercise," Jessie said.

"That's right. The two of you need all the time together you can get," Mrs. Wiley agreed.

Kate turned around and glared first at her mother, then at Jessie, and then at Dara. "Fine," she said. "I'll take Spy on the trails. Is there anything else you want me to do with him? Keep him in my room, maybe?"

"Kate," Mrs. Wiley began, her voice belying the fact that her patience was at an end.

"But first I'm going to finish these dishes," Kate said before her mother could say any more. "I'll meet you in the barn."

Dara stared at Kate's back and Mrs. Wiley's set features and thought how strange it was to see Kate and her mother at odds. Jessie grabbed Dara's arm quickly and started moving her toward the door. "We'll get them tacked up," she said in a falsely cheery tone. "Don't be too long, Kate. C'mon, Dara."

Anne Wiley met Dara's gaze and, hiding her own upset, came over to pat her shoulder. "It's okay," she whispered to Dara. "Whatever you decide about your training is all right."

"I bet Kate doesn't come," Dara said as they walked purposefully toward the barn, Jessie's hand still clamped to Dara's arm. "I've apologized to her mother, what more does she want?"

"She'll come," Jessie said, "cool down."

Arpeggio was waiting at the door of his stall when Dara got to him. He nuzzled her shoulder affectionately. She cross-tied him in the aisle and brushed him vigorously. Up close she could see how healthy his coat looked, but from a few feet back the shine disappeared. It was because he was a gray. A gray or white coat simply didn't reflect light the way a bay or chestnut did. She looked down the aisle at Night Owl, whose deep bay coat shone even in the dim light. Northern Spy's chestnut coat was even more spectacular. On a sunny day he looked as if he were generating light all by himself.

Dara and Jessie finished the grooming ritual and Kate had still not arrived. "I told you," Dara said to Jessie.

"Look, you take Spy out and start brushing him, and I'll get Kate."

"If you have to drag her out here, forget it," Dara said, wondering what good it would do to have them all go on a trail ride if Kate was determined to be mad at her.

Dara cross-tied the big chestnut and had him completely brushed before Kate arrived. Jessie wasn't exactly pulling Kate, but she was definitely urging her on. "Thanks," Kate said curtly when she took over the rest of Spy's grooming from Dara. They saddled up and turned the horses toward the trails.

"Isn't it a great day?" Jessie said, looking up at the sky, which was a hazy, dull gray. A few minutes later she asked Dara how her brother was doing. A few minutes after that she asked Kate if she and Pete had been to the movies lately. When they'd ridden clear across the fields separating Windcroft from the woods, and Kate and Jessie hadn't answered her with more than "yes" or "no," Jessie reined Night Owl to a halt. "Look, you two, I'm not going to spend the rest of the ride trying to keep a conversation going."

"Then don't talk," Kate said. "Let's just ride."

"I said I was sorry," Dara told Kate. "What else do you want me to do?"

"I don't want you to do anything," Kate said.

"Fine," Dara said coldly. "I won't."

"Oh, you guys," Jessie said. "You're going to ruin everything."

"It's just—" Kate began at the same time Dara said, "My riding—" Jessie stopped them both.

"Hold it," Jessie said. "Let's not start all over again. If there's something wrong with Dara's riding, then Dara should talk about it with her mom and maybe your mom, Kate. I don't think we should discuss it. Maybe it'll turn out that your mom isn't the right coach for Dara, but as your mother said, that doesn't have to affect *our* friendship, does it?"

Are you kidding? Dara wanted to ask Jessie. Of course it affects our friendship. Just like it affected all the friendships Dara had seen go to pieces at Concordia. The balance had changed. Kate on Spy had caused that, and it wasn't even Kate's fault. Could she help it if now she had a super horse to ride? The easy camaraderie they'd had was gone, and from now on it would be deadly earnest competition. Dara was no longer a natural, able to win simply by being there, able to smile when she didn't win because she knew it was just a fluke. She had passed the point in her training when new skills just fell into place. The skills she would have to perfect now were harder— she'd had a taste of that at Tommy's clinic. The problem was, she admitted to herself, that she had never learned how to work hard. At least not the way Kate was able to work. Keeping at it and keeping at it until the skill was mastered. Kate knew how to do it and Dara had never had to learn.

It scared Dara to death to think that she might turn into one of those kids she'd always disliked. Watching Kate, wishing her well, and all the time hoping that she'd fail. Because if Kate succeeded too many times, and Dara failed too many times, it would be good-bye Arpeggio. "I hate it, I hate it," Dara said to herself. She put her heels to Arpeggio and sent him into a startled run that took him along the trail and into the woods.

"Hey, Cooper," Jessie called. "Slow down."

Dara ignored her. At the point in the woods where the trail split into a Y, Dara turned right. This right-hand trail was Dara's favorite. The woods thinned and the trail widened for a long time, making it possible to canter and even gallop the horses safely. And just around a bend ahead there was a nice series of jumps they could take.

Dara heard Night Owl and Spy pounding along behind her. Ahead of them, blocking the trail, was a gate with a sign on it that said the trails on the far side were for the use of Ridge Trail Association members only. Since Windcroft was part of the association, Dara jumped the obstacle with a clear conscience and went thundering on.

Beneath her, Arpeggio's muscles stretched and contracted as his powerful stride sent them galloping down the path, the trees to either side no more than a blur. Dara felt the excitement that always filled her when she let Arpeggio run. She let it blot out all the unhappiness. It was the closest she ever came to throwing caution to the wind, to feeling totally free. Arpeggio's hooves dug into the soft earth, throwing clods of dirt behind them as he raced. The air rushing past Dara's face made her eyes tear. If they could just keep this up forever, run as fast as possible for as long as possible and leave every problem behind them.

Ahead the trail bent sharply, and her natural good sense caused Dara to sit back a little in the saddle. Arpeggio, sensing her restraint, slowed his pace, and Dara pulled back reluctantly on the reins. Arpeggio negotiated the bend at a safe, controlled pace.

Ahead of them off to the side of the trail was a large pile of brush, left there purposely to be jumped. She checked him more, and the big gray slowed to a halt. Kate and Jessie reined in beside her.

"Are you crazy?" Jessie asked Dara breathlessly. "What did you take off like that for?"

"Because I wanted to," Dara said, and sighed because she knew in her heart that no matter how far or fast you ran, what you were running from usually caught up with you. She turned back in the saddle to look at the brush pile off to the side. "Do you want to jump it?" she asked.

"No," Jessie said. "It's too wide and too high."

"How about you?" Dara said to Kate.

Kate gave Dara a measuring look and said, "Sure."

Dara watched as Kate estimated the approach, circled Spy back, and then sent him toward the jump. Dara watched the grace with which Spy ran, the powerful thrust of his quarters, the alert carriage of his head, the intense concentration visible in every line of his body. Their approach to the jump was flawless. A few feet in front of the brush pile there was a dip, and Spy went into the dip and jumped from there. The dip made the jump a foot higher than the brush pile itself had been. Still, Spy cleared it with inches to spare.

Jessie stood up in her stirrups and whooped, making Night Owl dance under her. "That was perfect. It couldn't have been better."

"Thanks," Kate said to Jessie. "It's something I learned from my mother." Then she eyed Dara. "Your turn," she said.

Dara heard the challenge in her words. "It could be done better," she said.

"How?" Kate asked her.

"By jumping before the dip."

Kate looked at her. "That's crazy. You know what a spread that would be? Besides, you can't get a horse to take off that far in front of a jump."

"*I* can," Dara said calmly. "Watch. It's something I learned from the king of eventing back at Concordia."

She brought Arpeggio up to the brush pile to get a good look at it, then walked him down into the dip and back out of it. It was wider than she'd thought it was. She bit her lower lip. Maybe Kate was right. The distance from the edge of the dip to the landing on the other side of the jump made it a very wide spread. Too wide to be jumped safely? Dara hoped not, because she was determined to jump it.

"Dara," Kate called. "Wait."

But Dara was committed. She brought Arpeggio back down the trail, almost to the bend. She squeezed his ribs, clucked, and slapped the reins on his neck. "Go," she told him. "Go, go, go."

He took off like an express train and came blasting down the path. Dara maneuvered him onto the grass and directed him toward the jump. Several strides before the dip she gripped his sides more firmly with her legs and shifted her weight forward slightly, usually the only incentive he needed to leave the ground in a graceful arc and clear whatever obstacle was directly in front of him.

But this time there was nothing directly in front of him. The jump, which he could see clearly, was several strides away. Dara knew what he was thinking. If he jumped this little dip in the ground and then landed, he'd crash right into the jump. Dara agreed with him, but it was too late. It had been a stupid grandstand play. Changing her mind, she tried to halt Arpeggio's forward motion, but it was no good.

Dara had asked him to jump, and confusing as the whole thing was, he jumped. Dara, caught halfway between the forward seat required of jumping and the deep seat required to slow a horse, lost her balance, further upsetting Arpeggio. He faltered, came down just short of the brush pile, and stumbled into it, almost falling.

Dara was thrown from the saddle and landed on the near side of the brush. Arpeggio's eyes rolled wildly in his head as he tried to extricate his feet from the branches and leaves of the jump. Northern Spy, upset by all the commotion, tried several times to bolt, but Kate kept circling him, letting him run his energy out harmlessly. Jessie had dismounted, nearly falling over herself in her haste, but with no one to take Night Owl's reins, she was afraid to leave him.

Thrashing out wildly, Arpeggio finally freed himself and took off like a streak down the trail, the sound of his hooves fading away, one broken rein flying wildly over his shoulder. For a minute there was total silence, even the cicadas were stunned into quiet. Dara lay on the ground where she'd fallen, one leg bent under her, both her arms outstretched, her riding helmet a foot away.

Jessie threw her reins to Kate, who had finally gotten Spy quieted, and ran to Dara. "Dara," she cried, "Dara, are you okay?" She threw a panicked look at Kate. "Should I touch her? Should I move her? What should I do?"

Kate dismounted slowly, trying to keep the horses calm, and snubbed their reins tightly around a tree. "Don't move her unless she's conscious

and you can ask her if anything feels broken." She
came to kneel alongside Jessie.

Dara heard it all. Heard Arpeggio take off, heard
the girls' worried questions, but she couldn't seem
to make herself open her eyes. "Take the horses
and go get your father," Jessie said. "If you ride
Spy, the Owl will follow you."

"Do you think we'll need an ambulance?" Kate
asked.

"No," Dara tried to say, and knew no sound
came out of her mouth. She forced herself to take
a deep breath and try again. "No," she said weakly.
"Don't. I'm okay. I'm just a little dizzy."

"Oh, Dara," Jessie cried. "I thought you were
dead."

Dara's vision was beginning to return and the
dizziness was subsiding. She struggled to sit up.
"Be careful," Kate warned. "Does it feel like anything's broken?"

Only my pride, Dara thought. And that was
probably in so many pieces she'd never get it all
back together.

"No, I'm okay, really. I just had the wind knocked
out of me, and bumped my head." She sat up and
put a hand to her hair. Then she raised her head
quickly to look around. The motion caused a
white-hot stab of pain behind her eyes. "Where's
Arpeggio?" she asked, a touch of hysteria in her
voice.

"He took off down the trail."

"Oh, no," Dara wailed, struggling to stand up.
Jessie and Kate supported her. "I'll have to go
after him. Arpeggio," she called, taking a faltering
step.

"Forget it, Dara," Kate said with authority. "You can't go anyplace but to a doctor's."

"But Arpeggio," she cried, "what if he steps on a rein, or trips and falls?"

"I'll chase him down. You get up on Night Owl and Jessie can walk you back to the farm."

"I can't leave," Dara said. "What if something happens to him?"

"Now's a fine time to think about that," Kate said.

"He's okay," Jessie said soothingly. "Just scared. He was running on all fours, and the reins were broken too short for him to trip. He'll probably circle around and go back to the barn on his own."

"Are you sure?" Dara asked.

Dara saw Kate look at her and then at Jessie, the worry in both their eyes obvious. Then Kate climbed up on Spy. "I'll see you back at the farm," she said. "Take care of her, Jessie."

Chapter 7

"WHAT happened?" Mrs. Wiley called from the ring where she was just finishing a lesson. "Where are the other horses? Where's Kate?"

"Please, Jessie," Dara whispered. "Don't shout it all over the place."

"It's okay," Jessie reassured Mrs. Wiley. "Kate'll be along in a minute."

Mrs. Wiley dismissed her student, then left the ring to come running toward the girls. She looked at Dara's white face and unsteady balance and told her to get off Night Owl at once. Gratefully, Dara let go of her hold on the saddle and slipped to the ground. Her legs gave out from under her and she sat down.

Mrs. Wiley knelt beside her, holding up her hand. "How many fingers do you see?" she asked Dara.

"Five," Dara said.

"Now?" she asked.

"Three," Dara told her. "I'm all right, honestly. I'm just a little shook up."

"Will someone please tell me what happened?" Anne asked, looking impatiently from Dara to Jessie.

"Well ..." Jessie said, glancing at Dara.

"I fell off Arpeggio," Dara said flatly.

"You? You fell off Arpeggio?" Anne asked, surprised.

Dara took a deep breath and continued, keeping her voice level. "And he took off down the trail, and Kate went to bring him back."

"Well, the first thing we do is get you to a doctor, young lady," Mrs. Wiley said, standing up. "I'll call your mother and find out who she wants you to see."

"No," Dara said quickly, attempting to stand and feeling the pain in her head again. She sat still for a minute, then got to her feet as slowly as possible. If she didn't move quickly, she would be all right. "You can't call my mom," she said to Anne. "She's at a meeting someplace, I don't even know where. Besides, I'm fine. I really am. If you call her, she'll just get all upset over nothing. My brother borrowed her car and he'll be along to take me home anytime now."

"Dara, don't play games with this. When your brother gets here, you get to a doctor and have yourself examined."

"I promise," she said. She turned, moving her head carefully to look back toward the trails. "Where are they?" she asked anxiously.

"They'll be here any minute," Jessie promised.

Night Owl was the first to realize they were coming. He raised his head and his nostrils flared. His eyes were glued to the line of trees across the field. He sounded a ringing neigh, and from beyond the trees a horse answered him.

"There, I told you," Jessie said. "I just hope she found Arpeggio."

"She did," Dara said. "He was answering Night Owl."

"You girls," Anne said, her eyes on the start of the trails. "You know your horses better than most people know their friends."

"That's because they are our friends," Jessie said. She brought one hand up to shade it from the sun while they waited tensely.

"There," Dara said, pointing suddenly. "There they are. And Arpeggio seems sound. Oh, please," she whispered under her breath, "please let him be all right."

Jessie handed Mrs. Wiley Night Owl's reins and ran across the field to help Kate with Arpeggio.

"I found him just on the other side of the creek," Kate said when they finally reached Dara. "Are you okay?" There seemed to be genuine concern in the question, but Dara was too worried about Arpeggio to acknowledge it.

"I'm fine," Dara said impatiently. "Is Arpeggio?"

"He's got a bad cut on his leg," Kate said. "It's bleeding quite a bit. I think it may have to be stitched."

Dara braced herself, trying not to see the ugly dark stain on his right front leg, and made her way unsteadily toward her horse. He lowered his head and pricked his ears toward her. She wrapped her arms around his neck and hugged him. "I'm so sorry," she said softly. "I'm so sorry. I wish it were I who had the cut. But we'll get it fixed." She was filled with a rush of love for the big gray horse who had never been anything but honest and loyal to her, and she had failed him.

She had tried since she'd gotten him to keep this intense love stopped up. What good was it to love an animal that wasn't really yours? That in a very real sense belonged more to your parents than to you? That at any moment could be taken away from you? But it was no good. All the love she had for Arpeggio came rushing out and she hugged him hard, her tears rolling down her cheeks and onto his neck. She glanced up to find Kate looking at her oddly.

"Mrs. Wiley," Dara said, amazed at how cool her voice sounded considering the torment going on inside her. "Would you please call the vet?"

"Sure, honey," Mrs. Wiley said from where she knelt, examining the cut. "It's deep and Kate is right, it will need to be stitched, but I don't think it's anything to worry about. See for yourself."

"I can't," Dara said, turning her head away. "I can't look."

"You come inside," Mrs. Wiley said sternly, taking Dara by the arm, "and lie down until your brother gets here. Jessie and Kate can take care of the horses." She turned her head to give the girls instructions. "Arpeggio's leg should be washed and disinfected. Then spray the area with that aerosol antibiotic that Dr. Rosen left us. Don't use any ointment on him. If he has to be stitched, an ointment will make it difficult."

"I should be doing that," Dara said.

"You should be lying down," Anne told her, and putting her arm around Dara, walked her to the house.

Dr. Rosen, the veterinarian, got there before Matthew, and Dara insisted on going out to the barn to talk to him. "It's not an especially bad cut, no tendons are affected," the veterinarian said, "but it is in a difficult place. Any cut on a horse's leg has to be watched because it's impossible to immobilize a leg. Every time he moves it, he stands the chance of opening it up again. So the big thing is to keep the wound free of infection until it has healed completely, and then he'll be as good as new.

"I've given him a tranquilizer. We'll give it a few minutes to take effect, and then I'll suture him. I'll need you to give me a hand."

"Let me help you," Jessie said quickly, eyeing Dara's pale face.

"Fine," Dr. Rosen agreed. "You're the young lady who has plans of becoming a vet, aren't you?"

"Hopes is a better word," Jessie said, smiling.

Dara's attention was drawn to some noise outside. Looking out the barn door, she saw Matt pull in, easing the car to a stop under the oak.

"You'd better get home," Anne said when she saw Matt. "And don't forget. You're just as important as Arpeggio is. We have him taken care of, you get yourself checked out."

"I will," Dara said. She started for the door, then turned around. Kate and Jessie were stroking Arpeggio's neck, and telling him to relax. Mrs. Wiley was kneeling alongside Dr. Rosen, watching while he gently fingered the wound. "Thanks, all of you," Dara said. But the words were spoken so softly they didn't hear.

"What happened to you?" Matt asked when Dara climbed into the car.

"I fell off Arpeggio," she said.

"You did what?" he asked, laughing.

"I fell off," she said defensively. "Lots of people do that."

"You're not lots of people," he said. "But I'm glad to hear you're not perfect."

"Matt," she said, close to tears, close to letting down the guard she had put up around her emotions, "how can you say that?"

He looked at her quickly and reached to pat her leg. "Hey, I didn't mean it the way it sounded, it was a stupid thing to say. I'm not happy you fell off your horse, it's just that finally I'm not the only goof-up in the family."

Dara looked out the window. "Well, that's a true statement," she said miserably.

When she got home, she went upstairs, took a shower, and lay down to rest, promising herself that she would tell her mother about the accident the minute she heard her come in. But Dara must have fallen asleep, and when she awoke, it was after five. She sat up in bed, her head pounding and her mouth tasting as if the gym class had marched through it. She brushed her teeth, then, gathering her courage, went downstairs.

Her father was sitting in the den reading the newspaper. He lowered it when Dara came in. "Hi," he said, surprised. "I didn't know you were home."

"I was upstairs," Dara said. "I was lying down."

"Are you sick?" her father said with concern.

"No. Is Mom around?"

"She's in the kitchen getting us some iced tea. What's the matter, honey?"

"Something happened today," Dara said, "but I'd rather wait until Mom comes in so I don't have to go through it twice."

"Barbara," Mr. Cooper called to his wife. "Can you come in here a minute?" His worried eyes were on Dara.

"Coming," she said, and in a minute appeared with two glasses of iced tea.

"Dara," she said, surprised. "Have you been home all this time? Do you want some iced tea?"

Dara shook her head. "Mom, I have something to tell you. I had some bad luck today. There was an accident."

"Did you have an accident?" her mother asked, raising her eyebrows. "Or was it Matt? I warned you about letting him drive your car. Don't look so upset, Dara, fenders can be fixed."

"It's not the car, and Matt had nothing to do with what happened." Dara moved uncomfortably in her chair. "I had an accident on Arpeggio."

Mrs. Cooper's hand flew to her throat. "Arpeggio?" She stared at Dara. "What happened?"

"We were out on the trails, and we jumped a brush pile." Dara paused and sighed. "I didn't plan the jump too well."

"And?" Mrs. Cooper had put her drink down on the coffee table and was leaning forward.

"And he didn't make it. I fell off, and Arpeggio went crashing through the brush. He cut himself pretty badly. It had to be stitched."

"Who stitched him?" Mrs. Cooper asked. "I hope you called a vet."

"Dr. Rosen stitched him," Dara said. "He's going to be fine, Mom. We just have to be careful that the cut doesn't get infected."

"How long will it take him to be 'fine'?" She paused for a moment as the information sank in. "Does that mean you'll miss the Waterfall competition? Will you have to withdraw from the rest of the season?"

"Mom, please," Dara said. Without thinking, she raised her hand to her head.

"What about you?" her father cut in sharply. "What did the doctor say about you?"

"I haven't seen a doctor yet," Dara admitted.

Mr. Cooper lowered his head and took a breath as if he were trying to keep his anger under control. "There's something very wrong in a house where the horse sees the doctor and the rider doesn't." He got up from the chair. "C'mon," he said.

"Where are we going?" Dara asked.

"To the emergency room. You need to be checked out immediately."

It was after seven by the time they got back. Matt was waiting for them in the kitchen, where he'd set the table and put out some cold meat and salads.

"Thank you, Matt," Mrs. Cooper said. "That was thoughtful."

"How's Dara?" he asked.

"I'm fine," Dara said. "I knew there was nothing wrong with me."

"He didn't give you a clean bill of health, young lady. He said you were to stay in bed until the headache stopped and then you were to take it easy for at least a week," her father said.

"That won't be hard," Dara said morosely. "There's nothing to do and no one to do it with."

Mr. Cooper paced back and forth, then continued. "This whole riding thing has gotten out of hand," he said, his voice growing angrier as he spoke. "I haven't been happy about it from the beginning."

"Oh, John," Mrs. Cooper said. "Don't get all upset."

"All upset? Dara could have been killed out there today. Don't you realize that?"

"Arpeggio's the one who got hurt," Mrs. Cooper said, trying to sound reasonable.

"And that's another thing," Mr. Cooper said, almost shouting now. "Do you have any idea how much money we have tied up in that animal? What if he'd broken a leg and we'd had to shoot him? We'd have been out thousands of dollars. That is not sound fiscal practice! That's it. I'm putting my foot down. I should have done it a long time ago. That's the end of Dara's riding."

"John, you can't mean that," Mrs. Cooper gasped.

"I do mean it," he told her.

"But this sort of thing happens all the time. You can't ask me to sell Arpeggio." Mrs. Cooper sounded close to tears.

"I'm not asking you, I'm telling you. I know how much you enjoy Dara's riding, but the fun and games are over," Mr. Cooper said.

"But all the time ... all the effort ..."

"I don't want to hear it. My mind is made up."

"Well, I won't hear of selling him. Dara and Arpeggio are stars."

Dara listened to the argument between her parents. It was the only time she'd ever heard them fight, and it frightened her. Even her parents were being pulled apart by her riding. Her dad was right; the fun and games were over. "Sell him," she said.

"Dara!" Her mother stared at her in astonishment. "That is the most ridiculous thing you have ever said. If you can't add anything reasonable to this discussion, then don't say anything at all."

"I mean it," Dara looked squarely at her father. "I'm sick to death of riding." Her mother was shocked into silence. "I don't care if I never get on a horse again." She turned and fled from the room.

The loud voices downstairs continued for some time, then everything was quiet. She heard footsteps on the stairs and a knock at her door. Matt opened it a crack and stuck his head in.

"Have they calmed down yet?" Dara asked.

"I don't know," Matt said, smiling kindly at her. "I bowed out myself. I have a present for you. Room service," he said, pushing the door completely open and bringing a tray into the room. "Le peanut butter," he said, "le grape jelly, and le vintage glass of milk."

"Thanks," Dara said, forcing herself to a sitting position.

Matt handed a sandwich to Dara and took the second one on the tray for himself. They ate in a companionable silence, and then Matt said, "Do you want to talk about it?"

"No. As a matter of fact, I don't want to talk at all. What I want to do is sleep ... for a month if I can manage it."

"I can take a hint." He kissed Dara on the forehead and picked up the tray. "But it's not always a good idea to keep stuff to yourself." He started for the door and then remembered something. "Hey, by the way, when I had your car downtown today, I met Mr. Wonderful." Dara turned quickly to look at him and was rewarded by another sharp stab of pain. "When I came out of the mall he was sitting in the front seat," Matt said, "and when he saw me, he was pretty confused. He was waiting for you to come out."

She stared at her brother. What had Doug expected? If she'd been there, did he think she would act as if nothing had happened?

"I liked him," Matt said.

"Good," Dara said, looking away. "Then *you* can be his friend. It'll give you something to do this summer. You didn't say anything about Gloria, did you?" Her eyes flicked back to Matt's face.

"Not a word," Matt said. "He asked me to have you call him. He said he'd called here all day yesterday and never got an answer."

"You call him," Dara said. "I'm going to sleep." She turned toward the wall and lay there staring at the small blue flowers in the wallpaper until they blurred and she fell into a restless sleep.

Chapter 8

THE next morning when Dara woke, the house was completely still. She looked quickly at the clock. It was ten-thirty. She sat up in bed, thinking, "I'm late." The dull ache in her head and the pain in her shoulders reminded her that she had nothing to be late for. No riding for her today ... no riding for her ever again. The thought stunned her for a minute, but she told herself the decision had been made. She got up and faced herself in her mirror. "It's not worth what you have to give up. Remember that! In the last week your whole life has fallen apart. Besides"—she looked away from her reflection— "you don't deserve Arpeggio."

She took a shower, dressed quickly, and went downstairs. Matt was sitting in the breakfast area with a buttered bagel on the plate in front of him.

"Morning," she said glumly, and poured herself a glass of orange juice.

"How's your head?" he asked.

"Hurts," Dara said as she sat opposite him.

"Want to talk about it now?" Matt said.

"No," Dara said.

"You know, I always thought you knew how to handle things. What happened to the old forge-on-ahead Dara? It used to amaze me how you could hold your ground with Mom, how you could have a difference of opinion, get it out in the open, and then go on being friends. Last night it was as if you weren't even there."

"I don't know what you're talking about."

"Didn't it occur to you that there was something odd about the argument Mom and Dad were having? I mean, you're the one who rides, you're the one who takes care of Arpeggio, but the two of them were arguing with each other as if the problem and the solution concerned only them."

"Matt, please, I don't want to talk about this."

"They're that way about my schoolwork, too." Matt ignored her request and pushed on with his train of thought. "Dad's always at me to get better grades, but he says things like 'I want to be proud of you, son,' instead of asking how he can help."

Dara turned her attention from her brother to the leaves of the maple in the backyard hanging limp in the muggy heat. "That has nothing to do with what's happening now."

"What exactly *is* happening now?"

"I made a decision," Dara said.

"Seems kind of drastic," Matt told her.

Dara shook her head. "I don't like what competing is doing to the rest of my life."

Matt looked at her. "It's not competing that's the problem. Believe it or not, I'm kind of competitive myself. The problem is Mom's insistence that you have to come in first. That unless you've won, you've lost. It's the same thing with Dad and my grades. So you see the two problems really do have something in common.

"They really think that I could get A's if I tried harder, and I know you do, too. What no one seems to understand is that I'm trying as hard as I can. It kills me to come home and have Mom and Dad think I spent the semester goofing off. I'm not as smart as Seth and David," he said, naming his older brothers. "I'm not even as smart as you. But I do have some great qualities. I just wish Mom and Dad could see past the grades. They don't tell the whole story. Just like a blue ribbon doesn't tell it all."

Dara looked at the misery in her brother's eyes. "You do have some great qualities, Matt. You're the best brother I could ask for. It would take me all morning to list the things about you that I love. And while our problems may have some similarities, there is one great big difference. I agreed when we bought Arpeggio that whether or not I got to keep him would depend on how many blue ribbons I won."

"It wasn't a smart agreement," Matt said.

"Maybe not," Dara sighed. "But it's the one I made."

"There must be a better way to solve this business than quitting completely. I'm sure Mom would renegotiate the deal if you asked her."

"Maybe. But that would solve only one part of the problem. The other parts would still be there."

"You mean the trouble with Kate and Jessie and Doug? If you want to tell me the rest of it, I'm

a good listener, and maybe together we can solve
it all."

"Thanks," she said, "but I've been over it forward, backward, and sideways, and I keep coming
up with the same answer."

"Well, I hope you're right. I can't imagine you
without a horse to ride."

Dara looked down without answering. She
couldn't imagine it either.

"I hate to leave you when you're feeling so
down, but I might as well get over to the mall and
see if anybody needs an extra salesman for a few
weeks. Mom didn't think my marks earned me the
right to spend August at the beach house."

Dara heated a piece of danish in the micro-
wave, took it out on the patio, and sat with
it in her lap, staring out over the pool. The day
matched her mood. The sky was gray and the air
heavy. All her mornings from now on would be
like this. Nothing to do, no place to go, unless
somehow she got back with Jessie and Kate.

She was trading Arpeggio for her friends. Was it
a fair trade? No, she told herself miserably. Nothing in the world would ever make up for the loss
of Arpeggio. But she was lying to herself if she
really thought she had a choice. She was going to
lose Arpeggio anyway. The days of automatically
coming home with the blue were gone.

For a minute Dara allowed herself to think of
competing against Kate on Spy, trying her hardest, winning some, losing some. It might have
been fun, but she'd never know. It was the losing
that would be her downfall. Each time she lost
she'd worry that this was the time her mother

would decide Dara hadn't kept her part of the bargain.

No. She was right to quit. The decision had to be made here and now while she still had something to salvage. She looked at the danish and her stomach rebelled at taking another bite. She went back into the kitchen, dropped it into the garbage, and grabbed her car keys.

Ten minutes later Dara turned into the drive at Windcroft and parked. In the ring Kate was riding Spy. She watched carefully for a minute and wondered at how far they had come in the last week. Inside, she knew that she didn't have whatever it was she needed to work the way Kate did. Kate, who must have seen the car pull in, paid no attention at all to Dara.

"I hope it isn't too late already," Dara muttered to herself. "It takes two to keep a friendship going." Inside the barn it was wonderfully cool, and the steady drone of insects, so loud outside, was muted.

Arpeggio was standing, one back leg bent, his head low, dozing. At the sound of his stall door being opened, he twisted his head far enough around to see who was disturbing him.

"Hello, sir," Dara said formally.

He looked at her for a minute before turning around and taking two steps toward her. Dara placed a gentle hand on his muzzle. "How have you been?" she asked him. He stared at her calmly. She ran her hand along his neck and back before kneeling down to look at his leg. There was a knitted stocking over the wound, and under it Dara could feel a bandage. The area above and below the covering looked healthy, free of swelling, and cool to the touch. That was good. It meant there was no infection. She knelt there, staring at Arpeggio's leg, then looked up at his patient face.

"I'm so sorry," she whispered. "It was such a stupid thing to do. You deserve somebody nicer than me. I promise you I'll find someone. I won't let you go to just anybody."

She stood up and looked him in the eye again. "Looks like you're going to be all right. I'm glad," she told him firmly, getting control of herself. It could have been so much worse. He could have fallen and broken a leg. They might have had to destroy him. Like the horse Mrs. Wiley had been riding when she'd had her accident. At that thought a chill went through Dara's body, and she shivered.

Outside on the path she heard hoofbeats, and a moment later someone led a horse into the barn. It had to be Kate, Dara hadn't seen anyone else around. Dara heard tack boxes being opened and leads being clipped and unclipped. She heard Kate lead Spy back outside and then heard the splash of water. Kate was giving Spy a bath right in front of the barn door—blocking Dara's exit. Well, the heck with that nonsense. Dara would just stay where she was until Kate was finished. Dara hunched down quietly in a corner, and after looking at her questioningly, Arpeggio snorted and went back to dozing.

Then she heard Kate's voice. She was speaking in the singsong way she often did to keep Spy quiet while she worked with him. "Once upon a time," Kate said to her horse, "there were three happy not-so-little girls. They all lived in a pretty little town in Connecticut. They were good friends, yes, they were. And they had a fairy godmother who saw to it that they each had a horse to ride, because these girls would rather ride a horse than go to a ball any day. One of the girls had *two* horses to ride. Some people thought she was especially lucky, but she didn't think so. Mostly because people kept pointing out to her how much better one of the horses was than the other. That made her very crabby."

You can say that again, Dara thought.

"Well," Kate went on, "one wonderful day followed another in the happy little stable. But everybody knows that fairy tales aren't real, and one day things changed. And nobody quite understood why. But suddenly the girls weren't happy anymore . . . they weren't even talking anymore. And one of the horses got hurt . . . and"—Kate paused—"nobody lived happily ever after."

There was a long silence, then Kate said, "Hi, Dara. How's your head?"

Dara stared at her sneakers for a long minute before standing up and walking to the door of Arpeggio's stall. Then she reluctantly unlatched the door and walked outside. "It's okay. Arpeggio's leg looks good, too. Thanks for handling that for me." Kate shrugged and went on brushing water over Spy. "I saw you in the ring for a minute," Dara said. "You looked great."

"Thanks," Kate said with no show of warmth.

"You know," Dara said, an undertone of anger in her words, "one of the reasons people don't live happily ever after besides the fact that the truth makes them crabby is that they hold a grudge."

"What do you have to hold a grudge about?" Kate asked, looking at Dara finally.

"Me?" Dara said in shock. "I meant you."

"I'm not holding any grudge," Kate said.

"Sure you are. I've apologized every way I know how for what happened in the ring the other day, and you're still mad at me."

"I'm not mad at you," Kate said.

"Oh, c'mon, Kate, be honest. You're hardly talking to me."

"Well, you certainly haven't gone out of your way to talk to me," Kate said.

Dara took a deep breath and said, "Look. Something's happened. I think it's going to solve a lot of the problems around here and maybe get things back to the way they were between us."

Kate gave Dara a long, searching look. "That would be terrific," she said sincerely.

"My dad is going to sell Arpeggio."

Kate dropped the sponge she was using and it fell into the bucket with a splash. "No," she gasped. "Oh, Dara, how awful. Why?"

"It isn't *that* bad," Dara said, struggling to meet Kate's eyes, struggling to hide her real feelings. "I've always known Arpeggio was just a way for me to get to the top. My dad's angry about what happened yesterday. He's never been crazy about my riding. And now he says I could have been killed or Arpeggio could have been hurt badly enough to be put down, and then all that money he has invested in him would be gone."

"But did you tell him that it was a freak accident? That you were just being stupid?" Kate paused and looked uncomfortable. "I'm sorry, Dara," she said, "but it's true. You were being dumb."

"I know it."

"Why did you do it? Anybody with half a brain could see that the jump was too dangerous the way you did it."

"Lately I don't feel like I've got half a brain," Dara said, falling into step beside Kate as they began to walk Northern Spy around the barn.

"Can't you talk him out of it?" Kate asked.

"There's no reason to try," Dara said. "In the long run it wouldn't make any difference. Nothing is going right for me anymore. My riding isn't anywhere near as good as my mother thinks it should be. And my agreement with my mother, when we bought Arpeggio, was that as long as I kept winning, I could keep the horse. Well, I have to be realistic. I'm not going to win events just by showing up anymore. After watching you and Spy, I know my chances of winning all the time have just taken a nose dive."

"You really can give Arpeggio up? Just like that?" Kate asked softly.

"I have to," Dara said, swallowing hard and keeping her voice cool. "That was the deal."

"But I never believed it. Is that why you're so matter-of-fact about him?"

Dara nodded, looking away, not wanting her to see how much the big gray horse really meant to her. But Kate kept staring, and eventually Dara had to look back. "You're not telling me the truth,

Cooper. Besides, how is this going to make things better?" Kate asked.

"Well," Dara sighed. "We won't be competing against each other. We can be friends again."

"You think that's why we're not friends anymore?" Kate said.

"I think it's the major one, yes."

"You're not only dumb, you're crazy," Kate said heatedly.

"No, I'm not," Dara insisted, getting angry herself. "I've seen it happen a dozen times before. Ever since that month at Langwald's, things have changed. I think it's great that he called you into his office and told you you were the greatest rider to come down the pike...."

"No, you don't," Kate said, her eyes wide. "You're upset because he told me that."

"No. I'm not upset. I really do think it's great. It's my mother who's upset."

"I can't believe it," Kate said, astounded. "Your mother? Dara, you've got me beat on almost every level."

"Then why didn't Tommy call *me* in?" she asked.

"Because that's not all he wanted to tell me." Kate stopped for a moment, not sure she wanted to continue. But she did. "The real reason Tommy called me into his office was to tell me that although I am one of the best riders he's seen in a long time, I'm never going to get where I want to go on Night Owl. He told me to sell Big Bird. And unlike you, I don't think of the Owl as only the way to the top."

Dara stared at Kate. "Why didn't you tell us?"

"Because I don't want to think about it. I don't

even want to consider it. And I'm sick and tired of everybody finding reasons for me to ride Spy."

"Am I one of the people you're sick and tired of?" Dara asked. "Is that another reason you're mad at me?" Dara said. "Because I talked you into it?"

"I don't know why I'm mad at you, Dara. I'm just mad at everybody these days."

"Me, too," Dara said. They looked at each other, and Dara could see a small smile flickering around Kate's mouth. "I'm mad at you, Kate Wiley, because you work so darned hard to be good. And I'm afraid that if I worked that hard, too, one of us would be so disappointed at losing, we couldn't be friends anymore."

"And I'm mad at you, Dara Cooper, because you *are* good and so is your horse, and nobody's after you to get a better one." There was a pause, and a grin twitched at Dara's mouth.

"And I'm also mad at you, Kate Wiley, because you have a boyfriend who isn't two-timing you behind your back."

"And I'm also mad at you, Dara Cooper, because—" She paused.

"Because why?" Dara asked.

"I can't think of anything else," Kate said, and they laughed out loud. Kate put her hand against Spy's chest. "He's cool enough to be put back," she said. "Let me do that." She walked Spy into his stall, gave him a pitchfork full of hay, and then came out to face Dara. "Well," Kate sighed, "I'm glad we got all that out in the open."

"Yeah," Dara said, and started to laugh again. "I was just thinking of poor Jessie. She was bouncing back and forth between us like a Ping-Pong ball."

"Are you mad at her for anything?" Kate asked Dara.

"Yeah," Dara said. "I'm mad at her for not being mad at me for something."

"Let's call her and tell her to get over here. We need to straighten out this business about her not being mad at either one of us," Kate said, and she and Dara collapsed into laughter again.

Spy, who all this time had been standing with his nose glued to the door, listening to the conversation, let out a ringing neigh, which was answered almost immediately by Arpeggio.

"They think we're crazy," Kate said, wiping her eyes.

"We are—were," Dara corrected herself. "We almost lost our friendship over nothing."

"We won't ever do that again, right?" Kate asked. "Well, now that that's settled, what's this nonsense about selling Arpeggio?"

"Well"—Dara's face grew solemn again—"I told you the story."

"And you're just going to stand by and let it happen? Look me straight in the eye, Dara Cooper, and tell me you can let him go just like that."

Kate stuck her face close to Dara's and waited. Dara looked at the concerned gray-green eyes staring at her, then looked down at the floor. "I can't," she said.

"I knew it," Kate said victoriously. "I saw your eyes that day he got hurt. I saw the love there."

"All right, I've admitted I wasn't being truthful.

Arpeggio means the world to me, but what good does it do to admit it?"

"Is it safe to come in?" Dara turned to see Jessie standing hesitantly in the doorway. "The last time I was with you two it took me the rest of the night to get over it."

"You're safe," Kate said. "C'mon in. Dara and I have talked it all out."

A bright smile spread across Jessie's face and she came hurrying over to them. "Well, it's about time," she said happily. "Now things can get back to normal around here."

"Not completely," Kate said, and filled her in on what Dara had told her.

"So your dad's going to sell Arpeggio?" Jessie said.

"Yes," Dara said.

"No," Kate said at the same time.

"There's no sense in talking him out of it now," Dara said in exasperation. "My mother's going to want to sell him after the next event anyway."

"Why? What makes you think you're going to be so awful?" Kate said.

"I told you," Dara said. "Nothing is going right for me anymore."

"What do you do when things aren't going right?" Kate asked Jessie.

"I try harder," Jessie said.

"Don't make it sound so simple," Dara said angrily.

"It is simple," Kate insisted.

"Not if you've never had to try harder," Dara said, almost embarrassed to admit it. "I don't know how to try harder." She raised hopeless blue eyes to her friends. "I'm doing what I've always done, and if that isn't enough, I'm sunk."

"You've never had to work at anything, have you, Cooper? Not grades, or riding, or getting a guy. Well, it's high time you learned."

Dara turned to look at her friends' earnest faces. "How can you stand to try?" she asked. "How can you stand to work hard, and take a chance that you won't make it? How can your pride take that?"

"Because my pride doesn't depend on whether or not I win," Kate said. "My pride depends on whether or not I do my best. I don't want to say anything against your mother, Dara, but I think she has things screwed up, and so have you."

"My brother said almost the same thing," Dara said.

"Do you think you could talk to her about it?" Jessie asked.

"I'd have to change her whole way of thinking. Do you know how hard that would be?"

"I would try anything before I just gave up a horse like Arpeggio," Kate said slowly. "You know what I think, Cooper? I think your mother ought to get out of your riding and into her own. Maybe it's time she lived out her own dream." Dara looked at Kate quizzically. "You've made it look too easy," Kate told her. "I think your mother ought to take some riding lessons. Maybe even get a horse of her own."

"Take lessons on Arpeggio?" Dara said.

"No, on one of the school horses Mom has for beginners."

Dara looked up at Kate, and a slow grin tilted

the corners of her mouth. "Can you imagine your
mother giving my mother lessons?"

Jessie laughed. "It might be World War Three."
Then she grew serious. "Maybe Kate has the right
idea. I think you should talk her into it. Then
she'd know how really hard riding is, and give
you some space."

"I'll think about it," Dara said slowly.

"Dara, please," Kate said, her warm eyes serious, "don't sell Arpeggio. Tell your father you've
changed your mind. Half the fun will be gone for
me if we don't compete together."

Dara stared at her friend. "You won't get mad if
I beat you?"

"Do you get mad when I beat you?"

At first Dara looked away, then she faced her
friend. "Yes," she said.

"Me, too," Kate admitted. "Does it make you not
want to be my friend?"

"No," Dara said.

"Well, there you are. *We* don't have a problem."

"It would be easier if the problem were ours,"
Dara said.

"Well," Kate said, "I guess it's up to you. Does
the fairy tale have a happy ending?"

Dara looked at her steadily and then said softly,
"I hope so."

"Remember," Kate said, cocking her head at
Dara, "even Cinderella had to clean the hearth
before she got to go to the ball. Which reminds
me of something else, how are things going with
Doug?"

"They're not," Dara said.

"Haven't you talked to him?"

"No," Dara said.

"That's funny. I saw him yesterday and told him about your fall, and he said he was going to call you. As a matter of fact, he said he'd called you a couple of times and you weren't home."

"You told him about my fall?" Dara said.

"Yeah," Kate stared at her with her hands on her hips. "What did I do, ruin your image again? You're not perfect, Cooper. Nobody is. Actually, once you learn to accept that, life gets a whole lot easier. Right, Jessie?"

"Right," Jessie said.

"I can accept it," Dara said. "I'm just not sure my mother can."

"Do we have to explain everything about life to you?" Kate asked as she ducked out the door.

Jessie and Dara sat in silence until finally Jessie asked, "What are you thinking about?"

"I'm thinking," Dara said, "that I have to explain some things about life to my parents."

Chapter 9

WHEN Dara got home, the house was empty, which wasn't unusual because Mrs. Cooper never did like to stay home. In Lancaster she belonged to a dozen organizations and clubs and was always on her way someplace, but like Matt, Dara wondered what her mother did here in Smithfield. Dara paused for a minute, her hand on the banister. Maybe that's why she had become so obsessed with Dara's riding these last few months. There wasn't enough to keep her busy here. If that was the case, then Kate's idea was even better than it had first sounded.

She took a quick shower to get rid of the earthy smell of the barn, put on her bathing suit, and went out to sit by the pool. The whole day passed and no one came home. Dara thought of calling the girls but decided against it. She needed the time alone to get her thoughts in order for her big talk with her parents.

Sometime during the early afternoon she called

Dr. Rosen's office to check on Arpeggio's condition. His secretary said that the doctor was on a "barn call" but would get back to her with a report. Dara took a glass of cold water out onto the back patio and sat down to wait.

Half an hour later the telephone rang and Dr. Rosen assured Dara that Arpeggio's injury, while not exactly minor, was nothing to worry about.

"Can I ride him?" Dara asked.

"Well," Dr. Rosen hesitated, "it would probably be okay, but it would be safer to keep him quiet for a week or so. Keep your eye on him, hose the leg down, keep his wound clean, and if that leg shows any sign of inflammation, call me."

It was six o'clock before Dara heard a car in the drive and her parents' voices. She called out a hello and heard her mother's rapid footsteps toward the gate in the privacy fence which hid the pool. "How is your head, dear?" Mrs. Cooper asked when she stepped onto the patio.

"It's fine."

"Did you go out to the barn?"

"Arpeggio is fine, too. Mom, can you and Dad come out on the patio. I need to talk to you."

Her mother gave her a wary look as if they had done too much talking already. Mrs. Cooper looked vaguely toward the house. "We were going out to dinner...."

"I really need to talk to you," Dara said.

"All right," she said reluctantly. "Let me get your father."

In a few minutes both of Dara's parents were settled in lawn chairs, looking at her.

"Dad," Dara began.

"You don't want to give up Arpeggio," he said.

"That's right," she told him.

"Well, thank heaven." Mrs. Cooper gave a sigh of relief. "I had no idea what nonsense you were going to come out with today. I'm glad you came to your senses. I told you it was the bump on her head that caused her to make those ridiculous statements last night," she said, turning to her husband.

"Is that what it was?" her father asked.

"No, it was more than that. I mean, *is* more than that," Dara corrected herself.

"So there's more at stake here than you being temperamental, wanting one thing one minute and something else the next?" her father said.

"John, you are handling this whole thing wrong. I told you that Dara hadn't—"

"Mom," Dara said kindly, "let *me* tell Dad how I feel. That's one of the things that was wrong last night. You and Dad were having this big discussion about my life, and I wasn't even part of it."

Mrs. Cooper looked at her in surprise. "I was just . . ."

"Don't," Dara said softly. "Let me."

"All right," Mrs. Cooper said, sounding miffed, "go ahead."

"I know that you and Mom love me, love all of us kids. And I know that you want the best for us. But sometimes you want more for us than we want for ourselves. I'm not sure about Seth and David, but maybe you want too much for Matt and me."

"Don't be ridiculous," Mrs. Cooper said.

"Let her finish," Mr. Cooper told his wife.

"Matt and I aren't perfect. We were talking about it this morning. Matt says he works twice as hard as any of his friends and he still can't get A's. It makes him very sad when you act as if he's a failure."

Mrs. Cooper turned to her husband. "Sometimes you are awfully hard on him," she said to her husband.

"And sometimes you're awfully hard on me," Dara said to her mother.

"That's *not* true," Mrs. Cooper said defensively. "I've never had to force you to succeed. You're always at the top."

"Not lately," Dara said. "And that's when the trouble started. You made being first, being the best, too important. And I probably made it look too easy, because in the beginning it was. But it's not easy anymore. If Arpeggio and I are going to succeed at this level, we're going to have to work hard for everything we get.

"And I'm not used to having to work to win," Dara continued in earnest. "That is something I'm going to have to learn. And, Mom, there are going to be times when no matter how hard I work, I won't win a competition. That's what happened at Langwald's. You won't help me by making me feel that because I didn't take the blue ribbon I'm a failure, or by saying if I worked harder I'd do better ... or by threatening me with selling Arpeggio."

"I never do that," Mrs. Cooper said, shocked.

"Yes, you do. Every time you remind me of the agreement we made when we bought him."

"But I would never sell him."

"How am I supposed to know that?"

"I just wanted you to realize that Arpeggio was something special. Something you had to live up to."

"I don't want something I have to live up to. That's too much responsibility. And if that's truly how you think of Arpeggio, then maybe my first instinct was right, maybe we should sell him." Dara said the words coolly, but inside, her heart couldn't seem to find the right way to beat.

Mr. Cooper was sitting back in his chair, staring at Dara. "Speaking from a strictly logical viewpoint," he said, "we spent a ridiculous amount of money on that animal."

"Dad, some things you can't put a price on. Arpeggio is one of those things. I've tried seeing him as just my ticket to the Olympics, but it doesn't work. He's so much more than that. I love him. We're a team. There's no way I can guarantee that we'll make it to the top, and you'll get back the money you put into him. All I can guarantee is that we'll give every competition our best effort.

"I thought it was the competition that was causing all the problems I suddenly seem to be having, but today I realized it isn't the competition that I hate, it's having to win that was driving me crazy. All those kids at Concordia that were clawing their way to the top ... I don't ever want it to be like that here. And it won't. Kate and Jessie and I will see that it won't." She paused and looked at her mother. "And you have to help, too."

"Me? How?"

"By letting my riding belong to me. Let me be as good as I can be and don't insist that I be as good as you want me to be. I know I'm doing something that you wished you had done, but I can't do it your way. I have to do it mine."

Mrs. Cooper gave her daughter a long, searching look. Dara held her breath, hoping she hadn't hurt her mother. "Is that what I was doing?" Mrs. Cooper said.

Dara looked down at her hands clasped tightly in her lap, the knuckles white, and nodded.

Mrs. Cooper was quiet again, then she looked at her daughter and smiled sadly. "If it's true, then I've turned into what I promised myself I would never be."

Her mother looked so sad that Dara wanted to rush over to hug her, but she sat where she was. "Well," Mrs. Cooper sighed, "now what?"

"Now," Dara said, smiling gently at her mother, "we all try to change."

"Easier said than done," her mother said, smiling back.

Relieved that her parents loved her enough to listen to her, Dara turned to her father. "So, Dad, you get the first chance. Will you change your mind? Will you let me go on with my riding and keep Arpeggio?"

"Honey," he said, reaching over to take her hand, "all I want for you, for any of you kids, is your happiness. And if riding and competing make you happy, then I'm all for it. I was just upset because you got hurt. Arpeggio seemed the easiest one to take it out on."

"That fall was totally my fault," Dara said. "I tried to do something dumb. But I'm a lot smarter now."

"Yes," her father said, looking at her with love. "You're a pretty smart cookie."

"And, Mom, will you agree to let me worry about my riding?"

"I'll try," Mrs. Cooper sighed, "but it may be hard. I love being part of the horse world."

"I have an idea that might make it easier," Dara said. "Actually, it was Kate's suggestion. I think you ought to take riding lessons yourself."

"Me?" Mrs. Cooper looked in amazement at Kate.

"Yes," Dara said emphatically. "You love horses, and you have the time."

"What an interesting idea. I suppose you mean I should take lessons at Windcroft, with Anne Wiley," Mrs. Cooper said.

"Yes," Dara said again, beginning to smile. This idea of Kate's had a lot going for it. "I think you'll find out two things very quickly. The first is that Mrs. Wiley is a wonderful coach."

"And the second?"

"Riding is not as easy as it looks," Dara said, grinning openly.

Mr. Cooper laughed out loud. "She really is a smart cookie. What do you say, Barbara?"

"Well," Mrs. Cooper hesitated, "I'll have to think about it."

Mr. Cooper checked his watch. "We'll have to get a move on if we're going to be in time for that dinner reservation. Want to come with us?" he asked Dara.

"No, thanks, Dad, there's someone else I need to talk to tonight."

Mrs. Cooper stood up slowly, looking as if she were still thinking about the things Dara had said. She was almost to the house before she turned and asked, "Did Dr. Rosen say when Arpeggio can be ridden?"

"He said I could probably ride him now but that it would be safer if I rested him a week," Dara told her.

Mrs. Cooper thought that over. "If he said he can be ridden now, you're probably safe in schooling him some. You have a lot of missed time to make up for. Waterfall is only a short time away."

"I don't think we're going to make the Waterfall competition," Dara said. "I don't want to take any more chances with Arpeggio."

"Don't be ridiculous," Mrs. Cooper said. "You need to get to every event you can if you want—" She stopped herself in mid-sentence and clamped her hand over her mouth.

"You two have your work cut out for you," Mr. Cooper said, laughing.

Mrs. Cooper smiled sheepishly. "I don't believe after everything we just talked about that I said that." She turned to Dara. "I just want the best for you."

"I know," Dara said, running over to her mother and giving her a big hug, sorry for how seldom over the past few years they had hugged. It didn't seem appropriate in Lancaster. But this was Smithfield, and Smithfield was definitely a place where Dara Cooper could hug her mother if she felt like it. And right now she did.

Looking over Dara's shoulder, Mrs. Cooper asked her husband, "And what about you? You've got some work of your own to do."

"You mean Matt? I'll see him tonight. You know, I guess both your mother and I thought that by setting high goals, we were encouraging you."

"I know," Dara said.

"I hope all this works out," Mrs. Cooper said.

"It will," Mr. Cooper said, walking over to put one arm around his wife and one arm around Dara. He led them toward the house. "Miss Psychology here"—he nodded jokingly toward Dara— "will see that it does."

Dara waved her parents good-bye and collapsed into a chaise longue. That had been one of the hardest things she'd ever done. She smiled happily as she went over the reception her words had received. She guessed that one of the things about growing up was realizing that your parents weren't always one hundred percent right. And when things went wrong, the best thing for everyone was to sit down and discuss them openly. For the first time in weeks she felt good. She felt as if she'd gotten her world back in order.

Now, if that other person she had to talk to would just be as reasonable as her parents had been ... She went to the telephone, picked up the receiver, and dialed Doug's number.

"Hi," he said. Dara couldn't tell from that one word if he was happy or annoyed that she'd called.

"Doug," Dara began, and then didn't know how to go on. This was very new territory for her. "I was wondering if maybe—" She paused. "I was just thinking that if—" She paused again. Then she was disgusted with herself. Too many maybes and ifs. "Doug," she started again, "I need to talk to you. Can you come over?"

There was a very long pause, then Doug said cautiously, "I can't."

"Oh. Well, that's okay. I understand."

"I have a practice match at the tennis courts. My time's reserved. I really can't get out of it. But listen," he went on hurriedly. "Why don't you meet me there? If you get there fast, there'll be some time before we play."

"Well," Dara said.

"I'd pick you up, Dara, but my doubles partner is picking me up and it's too late to change arrangements now."

Now she didn't know what to do. Would it make her look too eager if she raced over there just for the chance to have a few minutes with him before he played tennis? Well, she *was* eager and she *had* to see him. "Okay," she said. "I'll be there."

"Great," Doug said, and he sounded pleased.

"Hmmm," Dara thought as she hung up the phone, maybe things were going to work out with Doug, too.

It took Dara only a few minutes to drive to the courts. She was there before Doug. She parked her car and walked over to the series of outside courts. It wasn't dark yet, but the overhead lights were on. It saddened her a little to realize that each night it got dark a little earlier, which meant that summer was on its way out. A car pulled into the parking lot, and she recognized Doug in the passenger seat. She started toward him and was almost there when the driver's door opened and Gloria Skinner stepped out.

Gloria was Doug's doubles partner? Dara was devastated.

Gloria was laughing as she reached into the backseat for her racket and Dara imagined them talking about her all the way over. Doug telling Gloria that sophisticated Dara was racing to the courts to talk to him, that he had agreed to squeeze her in between sets. She stood frozen, fighting back tears. Her first impulse was to turn and run. Maybe they hadn't seen her. Let Doug Lyons think she'd stood him up. Then she remembered Kate and Jessie's lecture: "If something is worth having, then it's worth putting some effort into even if you don't end up the winner." And a friendship with Doug Lyons was definitely worth taking some chances for.

It was too late to run anyway. Doug was out of the car and walking to meet her. Her heart was jumping up and down in her chest like a yo-yo, and the closer Doug got, the faster her heart did those crazy loop-de-loops. When he was within a few feet of her he smiled, and his brown eyes crinkled at the corners. "Hi," he said.

"Hi," she breathed back at him.

"You look great," he said softly.

"So do you," she said honestly, her blue eyes glued to his brown ones.

"Ahem." There was a discreet cough behind Doug and he looked startled, then turned. "Gloria, this is Dara. Dara, this is Gloria."

"Hi," Dara said, intending to keep her expression cool and composed.

But Gloria gave her a big smile and said, "I've seen you at school. How's it going?" To Dara's amazement she sounded friendly.

"Okay," Dara said. There was an awkward pause and then Gloria smiled at Doug. "I'll be over at the backboard warming up," she said, and started to move away. Then she turned and said with a mischievous gleam in her eye, "I'd have stayed to get to know you better, Dara, but Doug told me if I didn't get lost as soon as we got here, he'd beat me into the ground with his racket."

"Thanks," Doug groaned.

"That's what friends are for," Gloria answered cheerfully.

"Well," Doug said to Dara. "I guess that kills the cool, suave act I was going to put on for you. It probably wouldn't have worked anyway. The minute I saw you I knew I was going to have trouble pretending I wasn't glad you were here."

"Why would you pretend that?"

He looked at her oddly. "Why? Because most of the time you're too busy to go out with me. You're never home when I call, and even though I asked you to call me, you didn't. It doesn't take long to figure out you're getting the brushoff." He looked directly into her eyes and Dara could see the hurt in them. "Have I been brushed off?"

"Oh, no," Dara said.

"Then I don't understand what was going on."

"You don't? How would you have felt if I'd asked you to go someplace and when you couldn't make it I asked another boy?"

He stared at her. "Well, it would depend on who the boy was, and how often I couldn't make things. If he was just a friend, if you had no romantic ideas about him, I wouldn't care one way or the other."

"Are you telling me that you and Gloria are just friends?"

"Sure. We've been friends since freshman year."

"But you took her to the junior prom."

"So? I didn't have a date, she didn't have a date, we went together. Did you think I was dating her?"

"Yes," Dara said defensively. "At least that's what Monica said."

"Monica? You listen to what Monica says? Why didn't you ask me?"

"Why didn't you tell me," Dara countered, "so that I wouldn't have to find it out from somebody else?"

"There wasn't anything to tell. It was like I'd asked one of the guys to drive out to Adventureland with me." Doug looked at her intently. "Are we having an argument?"

"I don't know," Dara said, confused.

"Well, are you mad at me?" he asked.

She looked at his handsome face, his straight, freckled nose, his warm brown eyes, and knew the feelings she had for Doug were a little confusing, but she didn't think mad described them. "No," she said, and started to laugh. This whole conversation was reminding her of another one she'd had just this morning with Kate.

"Well, I'm not mad at you either," Doug said, smiling broadly at her laughter.

"Then why are we shouting at each other?"

"Got me," he said.

"Doug," Gloria called, "our court's free."

Doug looked at Dara and said, "I have to go. Gloria and I are playing a tournament this weekend. But how about if we go out afterward? We can finish talking about Adventureland later. Or maybe do something more fun." He smiled at her.

"I think we've said everything we have to on the subject of Adventureland," she said, smiling back.

"Will you wait until I'm finished?"

"Doug," Gloria called again. "C'mon."

"Okay," Dara said.

"Great," Doug said, running toward an impatient Gloria. "See you later." He ran a few steps, then without checking his stride changed his direction and came running back to Dara. "I didn't just dream this whole thing, did I?"

"No," she said happily.

"Good," he said, bending down to kiss her on the cheek. "You stay right here."

Dara sat down on the grass where she could see the players and yet be out of the way, her hand on the spot Doug had kissed. Gloria and Doug were friends, that's all. And if Gloria's warm smile was any indication of her personality, Dara might even get to like her. Dara started to laugh. Wouldn't Monica have a fit if on the first day back at school Dara and Gloria came into the cafeteria arm in arm? Monica would have to find somebody else to gossip about, and that, Dara thought, knowing Monica, might take as long as three minutes.

Chapter 10

DARA turned fitfully in bed; someone was saying something about a concert. She opened her eyes and realized the radio alarm had come on. The soothing voice of an announcer told her that the His Boy Elroy concert scheduled for tonight was sold out. She leaned over to turn the radio off and stretched. Lucky she hadn't considered going, she thought, smiling to herself as she sat up in bed. Outside her window she could see a narrow band of gold light along the horizon. The sun was just coming up. It looked like a great day for the Waterfall Farm competition.

She got up quietly, showered, toweled her hair dry, and got dressed. She pulled on her creamy white jodhpurs, adjusting the patches of suede leather so that they were perfectly positioned against the insides of her knees. Then she slipped into her white sleeveless blouse and carefully tied the stock around her neck. She took a small silver-colored ring from her jewelry case and slipped it on her little finger. Doug had given it to her for luck. He said he'd won it at Adventureland and had brought it home to give to her. It was the first thing he'd ever won, so it had to be a lucky charm. She paused for a minute, remembering the kiss that had gone with the present.

She'd need some luck today. This was certainly a different kind of competition for her. She was riding Jonathan, Anne Wiley's horse, in a stadium jumping class. With Arpeggio laid up, she'd suggested to Anne that she help in retraining Jonathan. She hoped in some way that would make up for all that Anne had been through with the Cooper women this month.

Anne had agreed gratefully. Jonathan was proving harder to train than Anne had first thought he would be. And shaky as she was about jumping, she didn't want to pass any of her hangups along to him. Jonathan was coming along, but he was still somewhat unreliable and had a tendency to hesitate at and sometimes refuse a jump. Dara suspected he wasn't quite ready for competition, but she wanted to be there so badly, she decided to take a chance.

Besides, she told her reflection as she applied a small amount of eye shadow, and then a light brush of rouge across her cheeks, this will be a good learning experience for me, too. Opening her bedroom door, she caught the wonderful smell of bacon frying. She walked lightly downstairs and into the kitchen.

"Good morning," Barbara Cooper said, smiling at her daughter.

"Morning," Dara answered, surprised to find

her mother up. Mrs. Cooper scooped some eggs and bacon onto a plate and handed it to her. Dara sat down, drank her glass of juice, and started on the eggs. "You didn't have to get up," she said to her mother, "but I'm glad you did. This is a lot better than the bowl of cereal I'd have grabbed."

"Well," her mother said, sitting opposite her with a cup of coffee, "I can't change my entire life in a few short weeks, but I like getting up early. I like the excitement of event mornings, even though I'm training myself not to like them quite so much." Then she sighed. Dara paused in her eating and glanced at her mother. "Don't worry. I won't say another word about the fact that I'm not going with you today. I won't even say a word about the fact that you're not riding Arpeggio, and I won't say a word about the fact that you're riding Jonathan, though I can't say I really understand your reasoning."

"For someone who isn't going to say a word, you certainly got quite a few in," Dara said, laughing. "The whole thing is, Mom, you don't have to understand it, you just have to accept it. I know that Doc Rosen said I *could* ride Arpeggio, but I feel so responsible about what happened to him that I'm not taking any chances at all. I'll ride him when his cut is completely healed."

Mrs. Cooper couldn't help herself, so she said, "Dara, Jonathan is a klutz. You haven't got even a remote chance of doing well on him."

Dara laughed. "He is a klutz," she said, "but he's sweet, and willing, and he's learning. Besides, that's the whole idea. I haven't got a chance of a ribbon. This is a test for both of us." She fooled with her empty glass, then looked straight at her mother. "Me as well as you."

"Aren't you taking this too far?" Mrs. Cooper asked.

"No," Dara said. "And I hope you understand why I asked you not to come and watch today."

"I understand. Actually, not coming to watch you compete on Jonathan isn't much of a sacrifice. I'm almost glad I won't be there."

"Well," Dara continued, "I might ask you not to come to the next event, too, when I ride Arpeggio."

"Maybe I won't have time to come to that one," her mother said airily. "Maybe I'll be so busy with my own riding, I won't have time for yours."

"Your own riding?" Dara put down her fork and looked at her mother.

"I called Anne Wiley yesterday," Mrs. Cooper said. "I start my lessons next week."

"Mom." Dara's blue eyes were bright with pleasure. "That's great!"

"I couldn't stand not being around horses, and with all these new rules and regulations, I figured the only way to get back with them was to ride myself." She finished her coffee.

"Mom," Dara said softly, "I don't want you not to be a part of my riding, just not such a big part."

"I know." Mrs. Cooper touched her daughter lightly on the arm. She looked earnestly at Dara. "I really didn't want to move from Lancaster, you know. I was very happy there. But everyone else was so excited about moving, I didn't say anything. I guess I arrived at Smithfield with a chip on my shoulder and everybody paid for it. Your dad and I never meant to hurt you or Matt. We thought we were being good parents. I don't know what happened."

"You are good parents," Dara said. "The fact that we could sit down and talk things out proves it."

"That's true," Mrs. Cooper said. "It's wonderful that you had the courage to put us all to the test. But nobody ever accused you of not having courage. Did Matt tell you that he and Dad are going fishing today? In Rhode Island? Then Matt is going to stay up there for the rest of the summer. Seems he's got a girlfriend in the area."

"That's great!" Dara said, pleased for her brother. "And what about you?"

"I'm going to spend the afternoon at Windcroft, making friends with Miss Molly. That's the horse I'll be taking lessons on."

"You'll love Molly," Dara said. "She's a real sweetheart." She glanced at the clock and felt her stomach tighten with the pleasure of competition-morning tension. She was pleased to see it was there even though she wasn't riding Arpeggio. "I'd better get going," she said as she pushed her way back from the table.

Her black riding jacket hung in its plastic bag behind the kitchen door. Under it, in their flannel protective sleeves, sat her riding boots. She reached for her black velvet riding helmet on the shelf under the kitchen window and turned to her mother.

"Do you have lunch money?" her mother asked. Dara slapped the pocket of her jodhpur. "Okay then. Knock them dead," her mother said. Dara put one hand on her hip, and, raising her eyebrows, glared at her mother. Mrs. Cooper shook her head and laughed. "Do your best," she amended, and gave Dara a big hug. Then she stepped back. "You know, even though I agree with most of what we've talked about, there are going to be times when my opinion and yours won't be the same."

"I know that," Dara said. "And when I think you're wrong, I'll tell you."

"I know *that*," Mrs. Cooper said chuckling.

"But we'll be back to the way we used to be, when we could disagree and still be friends."

"We always were friends," Mrs. Cooper said. "It's just that for a little while we weren't speaking the same language."

Waterfall Farm was close enough to Windcroft so that they could walk the horses over through the trails. Dara adjusted herself in the saddle for the hundredth time. It was so strange to be riding Jonathan. He was a friendly horse, interested in what was going on. His brown ears flicked back and forth in response to sounds he heard around him. Ahead of her, in the shadows of the trees, she could see Northern Spy's shining chestnut rump, and behind her she could hear the steady clomp of Night Owl's hooves on the packed earth of the trail. She turned and smiled at Jessie.

Jessie smiled back uncertainly. "Stop worrying," Dara told her friend. "This will be fun."

"Fun," Jessie muttered. "Why do I do this to myself? I hate competing."

"You do not," Dara said, turning back to face forward. "Under all that complaining, you love it as much as I do."

They took the branch trail that led them to the back fields of Waterfall Farm and stopped for a moment as they came out of the woods. Ahead of them stretched acres of fenced paddocks. To the left were two big barns, and between them the indoor exercise ring. Beyond the fenced areas was a huge open field, crowded now with vans and cars, horses and riders. The scene was colorful and festive.

They circled right, walking the length of one of the fences, until they came to the narrow track that led between the paddocks to the main area of the farm. On their right they could see the dressage ring set out in all its precise beauty. On each corner of the arena was a large pot of bright red geraniums. Dara took a deep breath and inhaled the warm, exciting smell of an event day, a combination of horses, trees, dirt, and coffee coming from the refreshment tent.

"I couldn't have given this up," Dara said.

"We knew that," Kate told her matter-of-factly. "Let's register and pick up our numbers and times."

Kate had pulled an early number; in fact, she would be one of the first to compete. Jessie would be going almost half an hour later. "Well," Kate said, rubbing her hands together, "I guess I'd better school him a little. It's so different from riding Night Owl. I knew just what to expect from the Owl. I can't decide whether *I* want to win or whether I want Night Owl to win it ... to prove to all those doubters that he *can* beat Spy."

"And I think I'd rather see you win than see me win," Jessie said. "It's more important for you."

"Remember when you said to me it was hard having two friends to root for?" Dara asked Jessie. "I'm beginning to see what you meant." She was quiet for a minute and then laughed. "I bet you're glad that's over."

"Yeah," Jessie said, laughing with her. "Now we have Jessie rooting for Kate, Kate rooting for Owl, Dara's all mixed up, she may throw in the towel."

Kate groaned. "That's awful," she said while Jessie and Dara laughed. The sound of their voices caused Spy to dance in excited little steps. Kate reached down to stroke his neck and quiet him. "He's got this funny little hump in his back, I can feel it," she said.

"That's nerves," Dara said, looking at the exquisite chestnut her friend was riding. "Arpeggio gets that way, too. You'd better work it out of him, or when you get him in the dressage ring, he's liable to explode."

"Night Owl never gets like that," Kate said.

"If you say 'Night Owl never gets' again," Jessie said, "I'm going to choke you."

"Well, he doesn't," Kate said defensively.

"Come on, you two, let's get to work," Dara said, turning an obliging Jonathan toward an empty field. She relaxed into his easy trot and tried not to think of Arpeggio. They worked the horses, and then it was time for Kate to stand ready for her turn in the dressage arena. Dara and Jessie wished her luck, and then found a place to watch.

Dara loved watching the precise movements of dressage. It was a ballet on horseback. Kate approached the judge, saluted him, and circled Spy to the right. It seemed to Dara that Kate's test was excellent, especially considering how short a time she and Spy had been working together. There were some minor mistakes, but Dara could see that when Spy and Kate had developed a real working relationship, they would be a stunning pair. Spy was so beautiful, and Kate such an excellent rider that it brought a lump to Dara's throat.

They were almost finished. Kate was bringing him diagonally across the ring in an extended trot when he broke from the trot to a canter. Kate controlled him immediately, but it was too late. The judge had seen it. Kate brought Spy down the center line again, saluted the judge, signaling the end of her test, and exited the ring.

Jessie sighed, and she and Dara walked to meet their friend. To Dara's amazement, Kate was smiling.

"Well?" she asked, looking from one to the other.

"I think the judge saw the break," Dara said tentatively.

"He would have had to be blind to miss it," Kate said. "But except for that, what did you think?"

"Except for that, you were wonderful," Dara said, pleased to feel that she meant every word.

"We were, weren't we," Kate said, a happy smile lighting her face. "A few more months of training and this guy'll be unbeatable." Then her face clouded as if she didn't want to believe the words she'd just spoken. Kate turned to look at Jessie.

"Well, Jessica Claire," she said. "I left the door open for you and Night Owl."

"Thanks," Jessie said dryly.

It was one of Night Owl's better days in dressage, and when it was Jessie's turn to ride the test, they were almost letter perfect. There were a few hitches, mainly because Jessie, not the horse, was hesitant. And when she exited the ring she was smiling, too. "That's the first time I've ridden the advanced test," she said. "I was scared to death."

"But you did it," Kate said. "See, it wasn't so hard. I bet you can get Time-Out up to this level."

"Please," Jessie said. "I don't even want to think about it now. Talk to me next week, when I've got my nerves under control."

It was after lunch before Dara got the chance to perform. She had tried to get Jonathan interested in the jumps, but after a cursory look at them, his attention strayed to the dozens of strange horses in the ring with him. He acted as if it were his duty to make friends with every one of them.

"You will never be a champion," Dara told him, turning him for the twentieth time away from a small bay mare he seemed to be particularly fond of. She succeeded in getting him over all the jumps at least once for practice, and then the ring was cleared for competition.

Dara was the fifteenth competitor. When they announced her number she headed Jonathan into the ring, wondering why in the world she had agreed to do this. The horse was barely paying attention to her instructions. Dara circled him in a big circle until she could feel by his responses that he was at least partially listening to her. She

brought him to the fence and then turned him
toward the first jump, giving him a long approach
so that she was sure he would see what was
coming. It wasn't a polished performance. He did
see the cross bars coming up, but he waited for
Dara to tell him to speed up, then he waited for
her to tell him to jump and, after jumping, waited
for her to steady him.

The second jump was virtually the same. Dara
had the feeling that it might be easier on both of
them if they switched places, if she carried him
around the ring. Jonathan seemed completely un-
concerned. Dara thought if a horse could whistle
and put his hooves in a pocket, that's what Jonathan would do. The thought struck her funnybone,
and she laughed to herself.

Jonathan caught the sound, and his ears flicked
back toward her. "Come on, guy," she whispered,
"here comes number three."

Number three was a red-and-white bar jump,
with boxes of red, white, and blue petunias under
it. "It's safe," Dara whispered as she felt the brown
gelding hesitate under her. "I wouldn't ask you to
jump something that wasn't safe. I've learned that
lesson well." She tightened her legs around him,
squeezing tightly, asking him to go forward more.

The petunias were rapidly approaching, but Dara
could feel Jonathan pulling back. She applied more
leg, leaned forward slightly, and clucked to him
encouragingly, urging him forward in every way
she could think of. She could feel the exact in-
stant when he decided to trust her. His muscles
loosened, he took two strong strides, left the
ground, and cleared the jump.

Nobody noticed that the little drama had taken place. As a matter of fact, Jonathan was such an uninspired jumper, Dara doubted anyone had noticed at all. But she knew. And a feeling of pride went through her. Some sense of accomplishment must have gone through Jonathan, too, because he completed the rest of the jumps, then gave a little buck when he left the ring as if to tell the world how good he felt about things.

Kate came rushing up to congratulate Dara. "He jumped them all," she said excitedly. "He didn't refuse one."

"Yeah," Dara said happily. "I feel like I've won the Badminton Trials."

"What a willing little horse he is," a woman said, smiling up at Dara.

Dara looked down at her and then smiled a thank-you. Those were the words she had dreaded hearing, and now here they were not sounding bad at all.

That night, back at Windcroft as they put the horses away, Dara mentally reviewed the day. As it turned out, none of them were in the ribbons. Spy jumped clear in the ring and the inside course, but on the outside course he came in with a high number of time faults.

Night Owl had a good outside course but lost his concentration in the jumping ring. He decided he'd had enough, and try as she might, Jessie could not get him to complete the course. Dara sighed, remembering how upset Kate had been. Night Owl's spotty concentration was the biggest problem, and Dara guessed it was hard for Kate

to come to grips with what was obvious to everyone. If Kate wanted to get to the Olympics, Spy
was the horse that would take her there, no
matter how much she wanted it to be Night Owl.

"You did all right, Johnny my boy," she told the
tired brown gelding. She supposed she had done
all right, too. She'd gone to a show, ridden a
horse no one gave a second look to, barely completed the jumping round, got no applause from
the spectators, and yet felt good about things. She
had won something today. She'd won Jonathan's
trust. Maybe it wasn't a blue ribbon, but it felt
almost as good.

She closed Jonathan's stall and moved down to
Arpeggio. He was standing with his back end
toward her and didn't turn around when she opened
the door. "You're upset with me, aren't you?" she
said. "You can't understand why you didn't go
with us today. Well, I did it for your own good."
She knelt down and ran a hand over his injured
leg. It was firm and cool to her touch.

"I'm not letting anything else happen to you,"
she said, standing up and resting her head against
his neck. "You mean too much to me. Someday
I'll explain everything that's happened lately ...
when I understand it myself."

She heard the crunch of wheels in the driveway
and her heart did a happy little skip. "That's
Doug," she told Arpeggio, who grudgingly forgave
her her defection, and turned his head to nuzzle
her. "He means a lot to me, too," Dara said.

"Dara," Kate called in a singsong voice, "Doug's
here."

"I have to go," Dara told her horse, "but I'll be back tomorrow."

"Where are you guys going tonight?" Kate called from Spy's stall.

"Well, first I'm going home to explain to my mother that in everybody's opinion but mine my jumping round was mediocre, to say the least, and that I feel great about it. And then"—Dara continued in a happy voice—"I'm not sure. We'll probably drive around with some country music on the radio and then do something fun." Anything she did with Doug would be fun.

"Country music?" Jessie asked from Night Owl's stall.

"Everybody has their weird side," Kate said.

"Kate, does she sound smug to you?" Jessie asked.

"Yeah," Kate agreed, "but you forget, we're talking to Dara, 'the cool' Cooper, Smithfield's Golden Girl."

"That's me," Dara said, "a little older, a little wiser, but still very much a Golden Girl."

GLOSSARY

BIT: A metal or rubber bar that is fit into the horse's mouth to help control the horse's direction and speed; part of the bridle.

BLAZE: A striking white marking of medium width that runs down the middle of a horse's face.

BREECHES: Riding pants, usually of a tight stretch material, that fit closely over the calves and are worn inside riding boots.

BROODMARE: Female horse used specifically for breeding.

BRIDLE: Headgear consisting of head and throat straps, bit, and reins. Used for controlling a horse.

CANTER: A rolling three-beat gait, faster than a trot.

CAVALLETT: A series of long poles of adjustable height, support by crossbars; used in teaching both horses and riders to jump.

CONFORMATION: A horse's proportionate shape or contour.

CRIB: A type of bin used to hold food for stable animals; "cribbing" is also a bad habit of horses who bite the edges of doors, feed bins, etc. while sucking in air.

CROSS-COUNTRY: A timed event that takes place on open land. These courses include riding across fields, through woods, and along trails and require jumping over natural and man-made barriers such as ditches, logs, and hedges.

CROSS-TIES: A pair of leads, one attached to the right side of the halter and one to the left, used for holding the horse in place while grooming.

CURRY: To rub and clean a horse with a *curry comb*, which is a round rubber comb that loosens mud, dried sweat, and hair.

DIAGONAL: In riding, refers to the rider's position at the posting trot as the horse moves diagonal pairs of legs. On a circle, the rider would be rising in the saddle as the horse's outside shoulder moves forward (and the inside shoulder moves back). This keeps the rider from interfering with the horse's balance and freedom of movement.

DRESSAGE: Training a horse to perform with increased balance, suppleness, and obedience, and to perfect its paces. A dressage test involves a traditional system of complex maneuvers performed in an arena in front of one or more judges. The test is scored on each movement and on the overall impression that horse and rider make.

EVENT: Also known as a *Horse Trial*. A competitive series of exercises which test a horse's strength, obedience and intelligence. Also used as a verb: "Now she has a horse of her own to ride and *event*."

EVENTING: Also known as *combined training* and *three-day eventing*. A series of tests combining dressage, jumping and cross-country competitions.

FARRIER: A person who shoes horses; blacksmith.

FETLOCK: The horse's ankle; a projection bearing a tuft of hair on the back of a horse's leg, above the hoof and the pastern.

FILLY: A female horse less than four years of age.

FLANK: On a horse, the fleshy part of the side between the ribs and the hip.

FOAL: A horse under one year of age. Foals are usually weaned at six months and are then called weanlings. Also, to give birth to a horse.

FOALING BOX: A structure used as a maternity ward for expectant mares, usually designed with a gap in the wall so that labor and birth may be observed secretly.

GAITS: General term for all the foot movements of a horse: walk, trot, canter, or gallop.

GALLOP: The horse's fastest gait, although there are gradations; an open gallop is faster than a hard gallop.

GELDING: A male horse that has been castrated for the purpose of improving the animal's temper and health.

GIRTH: A sturdy strap and buckle securing the saddle.

GROOM: To clean and care for an animal. Also the person who performs these tasks.

HALT: In dressage, bringing the horse to an absolute stop with all four feet square and straight.

HALF-HALT: A subtle signal that encourages the horse to gather himself, improving his balance and preparing him for a change of pace or direction.

HALTER: A loose-fitting headgear with a noseband, and head and throat straps to which a lead line may be attached.

HANDS: A unit used to measure a horse's height, each hand equaling 4 inches. A horse is measured from the ground to his withers. Ponies stand up to 14 hands 2 inches (14½) hands high; larger horses are everything above. A 15-hand horse stands 5 feet high at his withers.

HAY RACK: A rack for holding hay for feeding horses.

HOOFPICK: A piece of grooming equipment used to gently clean dirt and stones from between hoof and horseshoe.

IMPULSION: The horse shows willingness to move freely, particularly through the powerful driving action of its hindquarters.

IN AND OUT: Two fences positioned close to each other and related in distance, so that the horse must jump "in" over the first fence and "out" over second.

JODHPURS: Riding pants cut full through the hips and fitted closely from knee to ankle.

JUMPING: In eventing, also known as *stadium jumping.* Horse and rider must take and clear ten to twelve fences in a ring. Penalty points are added for refusals, falls, and knockdowns.

LATERAL MOVEMENT: When a horse moves sideways and forward at the same time.

LEAD: The piece of rope or leather used to lead a horse.

LIPPIZANER: A compact, handsome horse, usually gray, originally bred at the Lipizza Stud near Trieste; famous for their use in dressage exhibitions at the Spanish Riding School in Vienna.

MUCKING OUT: To clear manure and soiled bedding from a horse stall.

OXER: A jump or obstacle that requires the horse to jump width as well as height.

PADDOCK: An enclosed outdoor area where horses are turned out and exercised.

PACE: The speed at which a horse travels, or, in harness racing, a two-beat gait in which the legs on the same side of the horse move in unison.

PALOMINO: Technically a color rather than a breed; a type of horse developed mainly in the Southwestern United States. These animals have golden coats and flaxen or white manes and tails.

POST: Rising up and down out of the saddle in rhythm with the horse's trot.

SADDLE FLAPS: Side pieces on an English saddle. They hide the straps needed to keep the saddle in place.

SERPENTINE: In dressage, a series of equal curves from one side of the ring's center line to the other. The horse changes the direction of his turn each time he passes over the centerline.

SHOULDER: A lateral movement in which the horse moves sideways and forward at the same time, bending his body around the rider's leg.

STANDARD: An upright post used to support the rail of a hurdle.

STIRRUP-LEATHERS: The strap used to suspend a stirrup from a saddle.

TACK: The gear used to outfit a horse for riding, such as saddle, halter, and bridle.

TROT: A two-beat gait faster than a walk, in which the horse's legs move in diagonal pairs (left forward, right rear).

WITHERS: The ridge between a horse's shoulder bones. The highest point above the shoulders where the neck joins the back.

Here's a look at what's ahead in TIME-OUT FOR JESSIE, the fifth book in Fawcett's "Blue Ribbon" series for GIRLS ONLY.

Jessie couldn't shake off the feeling that something was wrong at home. She tossed and turned for what seemed like forever and then she was dreaming . . .

In the dream, Jessie was at a horse show that was taking place in a clearing on the edge of a dense forest. The forest itself was dark and forboding, and the huge old trees with gnarled limbs and spiky branches stood like sentries, guarding its entrance.

Jessie strained her eyes to see more clearly. It was so dark. But suddenly lightning struck, lighting the forest, and then it started to pour. Thunder roared as streaks of silver flashed across the sky. The rain fell in torrents that slammed against the earth. It was then, at the height of the storm, that Jessie heard the voice of one of the judges.

"Time-Out," he ordered. "Approach the line."

Jessie simply couldn't believe her ears when she heard him call Time-Out to the starting box to begin her cross-country test.

"No!" she protested loudly. "It's too dangerous. The event must be canceled." But no one could hear her.

Jessie was even more horrified when she saw Time-Out suddenly appear, ready to begin. "Wait!" she cried. "Time-Out, stop!"

Nevertheless, Time-Out began the course, running in a state of terror. She took off down the trail at a gallop, all the time fighting off the needlelike rain that was blinding her eyes and lashing at her back.

Perhaps even more frightening than the vision of Time-Out was the recognition of her rider. Is that me?

Jessie thought frantically. Like the horse, the girl on Time-Out's back was in a state of panic. She looked enough like Jessie to make her think it was her double, and again Jessie tried to warn her. "I'm here. I'm Jessie. I don't know who you are, but I want you to go back. That's my horse you're riding."

The rider flashed a defiant look at Jessie, and she suddenly had the eerie realization that she was both watching her dream and at the same time was in it. The rider hung onto Time-Out for dear life as they stumbled along the slippery trail that led to disaster.

Jessie thought she heard the faint sound of snickering from two judges who stood up ahead of the far side of a ravine. Even though it was still raining, they sat on their horses, scoresheets in hand, seemingly laughing.

"Noooo," Jessie screamed, trying in vain to break through so that Time-Out could hear her.

The ravine was too wide, and the footing was slippery; it was impossible to tell what was on the other side. Time-Out took a frantic leap and landed on mucky, loose shale banking—ground that gave way immediately and pitched both horses and rider forward. Jessie felt herself sliding up and over Time-Out's back and down onto the sharp, slippery shale that pierced her consciousness and woke her up. . . .